SKATER
STUNTBOYS

SKATER STUNTBOYS

Pam Withers

WALRUS
BOOKS

Dedicated, with love, to Steve
on our 20th wedding anniversary.

Text copyright © 2005 by Pam Withers
Walrus Books, an imprint of Whitecap Books Ltd.
Third Printing 2007

Edited by Carolyn Bateman
Proofread by Joan Tetrault
Cover and interior design by Roberta Batchelor
Cover photograph by Annika Ridington
Typeset by Jacqui Thomas

Printed and bound in Canada

National Library of Canada Cataloguing in Publication Data

Withers, Pam
    Skater stuntboys/ Pam Withers.

(Take it to the extreme; 7)
ISBN 1-55285-647-x

    I. Title. II. Series: Withers, Pam. Take it to the extreme.
PS8595.I8453S53 2005   jC813'.6   C2004-907090-0

The publisher acknowledges the financial support of the Canada Council
for the Arts, the British Columbia Arts Council, and the Government of
Canada through the Book Publishing Industry Development Program
(BPIDP). Whitecap Books also acknowledges the financial support of the
Province of British Columbia through the Book Publishing Tax Credit.

We are committed to protecting the environment and to the responsible
use of natural resources. We are acting on this commitment by working
with suppliers and printers to phase out our use of paper produced
from ancient forests. This book is printed by Webcom on 100% recycled
(40% post-consumer) paper, processed chlorine free and printed with
vegetable-based inks. We are working with Markets Initiative (www.
oldgrowthfree.com) on this project.

Contents

1   The Carpenter

The late August sun beat down on his tense body and mosquitoes whined in his ear as Jake Evans bent over the narrow deck of his nearly finished half-pipe, drill in hand and a screw between pursed lips.

"Now, where the heck was I going to sink this last screw?" he mumbled as its metallic taste seeped into his mouth. Then, "Aha."

But as he poked strands of sweaty brown hair back under his baseball cap and lifted the drill to its target, two screeches made his body jerk around: the sound of a skateboard sliding down the metal stair railing behind him, and the "Yahoo!" of his buddy Peter Montpetit landing victoriously just inches from Jake's work-in-progress.

The screw in Jake's mouth dropped out, but a bitter, unwanted taste remained: jealousy.

"Jake, my man, it's comin' along, lookin' good. But

all work and no play can make a dude boring. Dare you to grind the rail fifteen steps, old buddy, one for each year we've lived. And we *do* know how to live, don't we?"

Jake, wiping sweat from his brow and casting his eyes on the grass for his lost screw, tried hard to keep his tone even.

"Peter, I'd just as soon make it to sixteen. I'm not ready for that rail. And if you hadn't noticed, I seem to be doing all the work on this half-pipe, even though I know you're going to use it as much as me."

Instead of prompting Peter to set his skateboard down and help, this only brightened Peter's smile as he stepped off his board and put a hand on Jake's shoulder.

"Never would I mess with the work of a master carpenter," he declared. "I'm all thumbs and no patience. Better that I be the official tester — and scope out the best places for us to do tricks while you're occupied. Think Sam will mind if I wax this ledge over here so it grinds better?"

In answer, Jake hurled the drill onto the ground and sprinted up the back steps of Sam's Adventure Tours' two-storey garage. But as he reached for the door, it opened outwards, nearly sending him tumbling.

"Oh, Jake, sorry. And hello, Peter," said Sam Miller, the bulky, red-bearded owner of the outdoor adventure company for which Jake and Peter worked. Sam let the door close behind him. "I see you put those spare pieces of plywood to good use. I don't mind you boys having a little fun on your time off back here. Maybe you can teach me a trick or two on those dangerous-looking boards, you think?" He chuckled at his own joke, tugged his beard, nodded at Jake, then hurried past him down the stairs to a dirt path leading to his truck. Mid-stride past Jake's construction project, he paused and peered at the half-pipe. "Jake, you built this with no plans in two days? I tell you, you've got your dad's gift. He was the best mechanic and carpenter I ever knew 'round these parts."

Jake felt his throat constrict, but before his face could burn with unwanted emotion, he converted it to a steely mask and exhaled slowly. Sam's eyes darted to Jake and quickly away, as if he knew he'd said something wrong. Then he smiled overly wide.

"You boys been hearing rumors about a big-name stunt coordinator from Los Angeles coming to town this week?"

Jake, still smarting from the mention of his dad, merely shuffled his feet on the landing.

"We've heard stuff," Peter enthused as he plunked down on the bottom step. "What's going on with that?"

"Well, I'll let you be the first to know. He's hired Sam's Adventure Tours to coordinate stunt work for a low-budget sports-action movie. It'll be his debut as a director. There's whitewater rafting and heli-skiing in it, even skateboarding. We're doing logistics for the stuntmen on the whitewater rafting and skiing parts."

"Skateboarding?" Peter's voice cracked with excitement, prompting Jake to roll his eyes. Here it comes, he thought: Peter who aspires to be a movie star and has the looks for it, Peter the all-around athlete who never lacks for confidence or energy. He's imagining himself the star of a film with skateboarding in it less than a nanosecond after hearing of it.

"Where are they filming the skateboarding, Sam?" Peter pressed as Jake held his tongue. "Are they using any local skateboarders? And why here in Chilliwack, British Columbia?" Peter was visiting from Seattle, just south.

Sam smiled. "At the massive, private indoor skatepark they're building across town, of course. Yeah, they're doing tryouts for stuntboys. And why here? Well, besides the fact that your fellow Americans like the way your dollars stretch here in Canada, you have to admit that this area has everything the movie needs: whitewater rivers, snow-capped peaks even in summer, and a spankin' new skateboard park. Not to mention a hardworking, reputable outfitter willing to serve movie moguls." He patted his chest in case they hadn't gotten that.

"But the skatepark isn't finished yet," Peter protested.

"As near to being finished as Jake's little half-pipe here," Sam said. "Gotta fly, boys. Stay out of trouble." With that, he hustled his bulk down the path with a silly little wave and another annoying chuckle.

"Gotta fly, boys. Stay out of trouble," Peter mimicked quietly in a high voice.

"Shut up, Peter," Jake whispered from the lower landing. "Stop being a jerk or you'll get us fired."

"Jerk? Whoa, old buddy, calm down. What's eating you? And whad'you say we cruise over to the new skatepark and see what's happening there?"

"Peter, we got Sam's permission to build this ramp behind Sam's Adventure Tours 'cause we weren't exactly welcomed by the toughs who seem to have staked it out as theirs, remember?"

"Yeah, well, if there are tryouts for movie stunts going on there soon — we could get *paid* to do tricks, Jake. Forget a couple of posers trying to intimidate us, right? We're as good as they are any day. That's probably why they don't want us hanging there."

"*You're* as good as them. I'm not in their league." Jake regretted the words as soon as they'd left his mouth. Trouble was, every sport he and Peter had taken on since they'd grown up next door to each other, they had shone at equally well. Both were strong and competitive — natural athletes, as their mothers liked to say. Even Peter's move to Seattle hadn't stopped the friendly competition between them. That had been the same summer Jake's dad had run off after a fight with Jake's mom. He'd disappeared without a trace and had never even written or sent them support payments. But the boys had kept in touch, had kept meeting up for sports events and adventures. Like this week: Peter was crashing at Jake's place before the school year would separate them again. But as much as skateboarding had become the boys' latest passion, for the first time, Jake was feeling outclassed by his best friend, and it was boring a hole in him. That, and the fact that next Saturday — a week from tomorrow — was his dad's birthday *and* the third anniversary of the day he'd disappeared. That double hit alone was making the week tense and sober for Jake, his mother, and his twelve-year-old sister, Alyson. But Peter had no way of knowing that.

"Jake," Peter's voice had taken on an earnest, hurt tone, "why are you so down on yourself? You could take those guys down a notch if you put your mind to it. You're way better than you think. You just have to want it."

Jake knew Peter was only trying to help, but the last words stung him with the force of a wasp landing twice. "Go wax your ledge," Jake muttered, grabbing the door handle, stepping inside Sam's garage, and slamming the door behind him.

He let the dim coolness of the place calm him. He felt his pulse slow, and the sweat on his body begin to dissipate.

"Hey," a woman's soft, gentle voice rose from a desk in the corner of the garage. "Wind catch the door? Not likely, since there's not even a breeze out there. Miserably hot today, isn't it?"

"Hi, Nancy," Jake greeted Nancy Sheppard, Sam's tall, capable manager as she rose from her office chair. "Sorry about the door."

"No need to hang around here, you know," she said. "It's Friday and you finished up hours ago, didn't you?"

"I'm just collecting my stuff to head home. Peter and I swept the garage floor and washed and vacuumed the passenger bus, and I changed its oil and patched those two rafts, like you asked."

"I know. You're amazing," Nancy replied, eyes searching his face as he paused, as if trying to decipher his taut facial muscles. "And made progress on your skateboarding ramp besides, I assume. Can I give you a lift home?"

"No, thanks." With some effort, Jake directed a grin her way. "I've got lots of wheels." He lifted his skateboard down from a shelf, buckled it into straps on his backpack, and grabbed his bike, which was resting against the wall. "So, tomorrow Peter and I are supposed to organize and mark the new snowshoes that just came in for next season?"

"That's right. That'll be just a half-day for you two. You may not even see me. Sam and I will be in meetings with a V.I.P. all morning."

"A very important person," Jake said. "I know. Sam told us."

"Did he? Yes, the movie director. Well, we'll know more tomorrow what it means for the company. Have a good evening, Jake."

He had a feeling she was about to add something like "Cheer up," but she wisely refrained.

Jake wheeled his bike across the freshly swept garage floor, out the front door, and around the corner. Once out of Nancy's sight, he leaned his bike against the building and whipped his skateboard off his pack. He had to wait up for Peter, he knew; he had to apologize for his grumpiness. But why not skate for a few minutes first, on his own?

He had to apologize to Peter, Jake told himself sternly, because Peter was his houseguest. And besides, did Peter even know about the birthday/ anniversary thing? Probably not, and it's not as if Jake was about to tell him. Jake shrugged out of his backpack and sat down on his skateboard. He stared vacantly at the thirsty grass of the big lawn. It sloped at a steep angle toward the quiet, tree-lined street in front of Sam's business, interrupted only by a set of concrete steps.

He sighed. During that dark first year after Jake's dad's disappearance, Peter had been so busy adjusting to his move to Seattle three hours south, he'd never really witnessed the turmoil forced on the remains of Jake's family. He hadn't been around for any of it: The initial expectation that Robert Evans would come loping back with apologies. The rising panic. The fruitless police search. The gradual shock, denial, and anger, and the unbearable sympathy of neighbors and teachers. It had all taken a toll. Jake buried his head in his hands. Worst of all had been the brief spell of highly embarrassing "Missing" posters and media attention. Eventually, Jake had bottled up both the good memories of his dad and the pain of his disappearance and swallowed them — sealed as tightly as a medicine capsule. Flushed them silently into the battered sea of his soul. How could he have known that the capsule would knock against his ribs annually like a ghost banging to get out of a closet?

Jake set his jaw, stood up, placed his feet on his skateboard, and began to rock back and forth. This week would pass. It always did. He just had to ride out the lousy feelings until it ended. People who'd lost someone to death must go through the same thing, this cruel and uninvited anniversary pain. He had more in common with them than they knew. But at least they knew, for certain, where their loved one was, and in most cases, they knew that it wasn't by choice that person had left and failed to return.

The roar of a passing motorcycle brought Jake back to the present. He looked at his feet positioned on his skateboard, and let it begin to roll. Steady, he told himself as his board slid toward the nine steps down Sam's front walkway, which he'd been practicing ollieing — in other words, jumping. Nine steps, three for each year his father had been gone without a trace. Nine ludicrously tall and deep steps of body-slamming hard concrete. If he could land his board this time, it would be a cool move, his best trick. He'd been getting close. If he could clear the steps today, he'd go back and make things right with Peter who was, after all, his best buddy. If he could jump clear, it would lighten his mood for sure, allow him to be as happy-go-lucky as Peter always was. Well, for a few minutes, anyway, he thought with a shadow of a grin on his face.

Shifting his left foot toward the front of the board, Jake crouched for a wide ollie and imagined that the board was super-glued to his feet. He shot up and over the steps, leaned forward, sucked his board up, and prepared to land both trucks (axle and wheel unit) on the pavement below. But the invisible gnome who inhabited the middle step of Sam's Adventure Tours' front walkway lifted his pudgy little arm and punched the underside of the board — sending him as usual to a crash landing. As Jake lay defeated with yet a new case of road rash, he was sure he could hear the gnome cackling.

A memory from eight years earlier pushed itself on him:

"Mom? Dad?" Jake, just off the school bus, clutched his skateboard to his chest, ran into the kitchen, smelled fresh-baked cookies, heard the deafening thump-thump of the dryer dancing in the basement. He figured she was down there, probably hadn't heard him. No sign of his little sister, either. Tiptoeing now, seeing his big chance to check out the secret in the garage, he slipped out the back door and sprinted across the backyard. He paused before the door that his dad had forbidden him to enter until tomorrow, his seventh birthday. It was quiet in there now, unlike yesterday, with all the hammering and sawing noises.

He knew he shouldn't spoil the surprise, but he had a pretty good idea of what it was all about, which is why he was cradling his precious skateboard in his arms. A gentle push on the door, a backward glance. He was undetected. And there, before him, sat two little quarter-pipes, just the right distance apart to play on. Reverently, he ran a hand along the transition, the steep bit.

Chest bursting, he climbed up onto his father's masterpiece with his board. He hadn't done this before, but he knew every move from watching the big boys at the local skatepark. He placed his feet wide apart on the board, which hung over the drop like a diving board. He closed his eyes, visualized the perfect dropping in, tilted his body a little sideways. Failed to notice a shadow emerge from behind him.

Oops. Leaned too far back. He began to dive, heading for a nasty, butt-landing, head-banging tumble. Suddenly, strong arms caught him, swung him up in the air, embraced him as his board clattered to a stop.

Jake clutched his dad's suspenders, rested against his ample stomach, looked guiltily into his face.

"Sorry, Dad, I ruined the surprise, didn't I?"

All he got was a glowing smile and a bear hug.

"Happy birthday a day early, Jake."

2   Sam's Backyard

"So," Peter said as he pedaled his bike alongside Jake's on the way to Sam's Adventure Tours the next morning, "Nancy said as soon as we've organized some snowshoes, we're off-duty?"

"Yup. She's in meetings all day with Sam and the L.A. guy." As Jake braked hard for a traffic light, he felt the tail of the skateboard strapped to his backpack jab him in the back.

"The guy shooting the movie."

"Yes, Peter, the guy who's going to discover you."

Peter grinned. "Hey, you never know. And then you can say you knew me before I was big."

"Big in the head? I don't think so," Jake teased back. He'd vowed this morning to make it through the day without being grumpy, but here he was, letting sarcasm seep through the walls of his happy façade already. The traffic light turned green, and they sped along, conversing in snatches when they could ride abreast.

"And what's your goal today, Peter? To help me finish the half-pipe?"

"Sure, why not? Then we can train up on all the tricks we'll need to look slick when we hit the new skate plaza this afternoon."

Jake stopped himself from saying, "You mean, look good in a showdown with the regulars there?" He awarded himself one point for his restraint. Then he thought, not for the first time, how strange it was that the just-completed outdoor skateboard plaza beside the giant, nearly finished indoor skatepark had already attracted a clique of local toughs doing their best to make others feel unwelcome.

"I guess when the indoor park opens and the new manager arrives, it'll be better supervised," Jake said. "I hear the manager is a young guy who used to compete big-time."

"I heard that too — a former X Games vert champion. For sure he'll tell those jerks who's boss," Peter said as they swung their bikes into Sam's driveway.

Jake shrugged. "Our half-pipe is as good as their little concrete plaza, and it's all ours." He stepped off his bike, fished keys out of his shorts pocket to open the side door to Sam's garage, then pressed the button to open the extra-high garage doors. As he did so, he breathed deeply of the familiar garage smells: gasoline, rubber from the stack of rafts, and glues and varnish from an assortment of containers. To Jake, who used to spend hours tinkering with his dad in their garage, the cool interior and "working smells," as his dad used to call them, were soothing. For the past two years, Sam's oversized garage, with its loft rooms at the back, its well-outfitted workbench, and neatly stacked sports equipment had been his sanctuary. This was his not-so-secret getaway, physically and emotionally, when the world outside seemed to spin too fast.

Peter entered, locked up his bike, and wrinkled his nose.

"Stinks in here, but at least it's cooler than outside. Gonna be a scorcher today." He switched on the only floor fan, hauled a chair over to it, and plunked himself down like a hotel guest awaiting a porter. "So where's the new gear for marking?"

With a look up at the loft's closed office door, Jake fingered the keys on his key ring and opened a nearby closet door.

"Whoa. Enough snowshoes to outfit the entire Arctic population," Peter observed. "Let's see. We'll divide these into two piles and see who finishes their half first."

It took the boys three hours to sort through, mark,

and organize the closet full of newly purchased winter sports gear.

"Hard to imagine Sam and Nancy booking heli-ski and snowshoe tours in this heat," Peter commented as his pile dwindled to the last few items. He leaned forward in his plastic chair to crank up the volume on the radio beside them. "What wouldn't I give for a little snow to roll around in right now?"

"Hmmm, we could sprinkle some on the half-pipe and do snowboard moves," Jake offered as he glanced upstairs and lowered the radio's volume.

"Hey! I'm finished," Peter said jubilantly as he scrawled "S.A.T." for Sam's Adventure Tours in permanent ink on the last snowshoe, and leapt up. "And so are you." The boys stacked the snowshoes back in the closet in towering piles.

"Race you to the half-pipe," Peter shouted as Jake closed and locked the closet door.

But Jake was too fast for him. He sprinted for the back door, threw it open, and vaulted down the steps one breath ahead of his rival. He'd spent enough time around Peter to know when his buddy was about to challenge him to a contest, and it wasn't in Jake's nature to lose. Panting, Jake leapt up onto the deck of the half-pipe first, then touched the lip. A sliver made him yank his hand away.

"Still needs coping. But it's pretty much there,

hey?" Peter said, sliding his own hand down the steep plywood.

Jake liked that the top layer of thin plywood was a former "Sam's Adventure Tours" sign that had just the letters "O-U-R-S" showing. They'd sure had to jump on that to curve it just right.

"What're we doing for coping?" Peter asked.

"Sam's got some old PVC tubing left from his bathroom renovation. He said we could use it. But I'm still puzzling out exactly how to lay it down."

"Awesome. Puzzle away, Engineer Jake; I know you'll get it." With Peter's help, Jake fetched the tubing, lay it over the edge where the lip met the "tranny," or transition, and sawed it to size. After some serious contemplation, Jake drilled large holes at intervals in the top of the tube, to allow him to reach through with the screwdriver to pre-drill smaller holes in the bottom of the tube.

"Good thinking," Peter observed.

After numerous tries and a few curses trying to get screws to stay on the ends of their screwdrivers, the boys managed to sink screws through the smaller holes until the tubing, nearly flush to the ramp, was fully secured.

"Sticks out a little at the top, but that's okay," Peter said. "Will the plastic hold up to what we'll be doing on it?"

"Metal would be better, but it should be okay," Jake said, giving a final twist to the last screw.

Peter climbed up to the platform with his skateboard in hand. "Permission to drop in, sir?"

Jake shook his head and motioned Peter to jump off. "No, we need to strengthen everything up." He pushed on the half-pipe and it shifted slightly, like an old man putting weight on a different hip. Jake peered around, pounced on two long two-by-fours, and hauled one over to a tree beside his project. "We're going to secure this end to the tree," he directed.

"You bet!" Peter agreed, grabbing one end to help Jake hold and nail the brace into place. They repeated the strategy on the other end, then pushed on the half-pipe again. This time, it held firm and strong.

"Now?" Peter asked.

"No, I want to do a final inspection underneath," Jake declared. He crawled under the half-pipe and eyed each and every two-by-four forming the ribbing on the plywood's curves.

"Don't know how shipbuilders do it," he mumbled aloud. "They have to bend the ribbing, not just the plywood."

"What's that got to do with anything?" Peter asked impatiently.

"Half-pipes, ship hulls, nearly the same design," Jake explained. "Anyway, everything looks screwed down tight. And the way we overlapped the plywood is good: no butt ends to catch wheels or anything."

"Yada yada," Peter said, rolling his eyes. Jake smiled. Construction technique might fascinate him, but no point wasting it on Peter. Peter was a man of action. Peter lived for the moment.

"Okay, let'er rip," Jake shouted as he scrambled out from beneath his creation and patted it proudly. It wasn't special enough to deserve breaking a champagne bottle over, but it was his biggest accomplishment yet, and he was pretty sure that if his dad were standing there, he'd unhook a thumb from his suspenders just long enough to give it a thumbs up.

Jake watched Peter smile and drop in like a pro, roll halfway up the far side, and let gravity and a relaxed stance keep pumping him until, like a pendulum now fully wound up, he felt ready to add a nose grab. As he caught air, Peter clamped his hand around the nose of his board, floated over the lip, then released his grab before his board landed again. After grudgingly admiring Peter's form for a while, Jake clambered up to the deck and dropped in to join him, carving a little hesitantly at first, then working his legs and knees to drive himself higher up the smooth, steep sides of his project. In tandem now, the two let their bodies swing — toes shifting, arms flying, elbows bending on cue, boards raising a fearful racket. So busy were they initiating their new plaything, the boys hardly noticed a bike pull up.

"Hi, Jake! Hi, Peter! You guys finished it!" Jake turned and smiled at Alyson. His little sister dropped her bike, stepped closer, and ducked her head under the half-pipe to inspect its undersides. "Wow. Can I try it?"

Jake hopped off his board and stepped on its kicktail to make it pop up to his hand. He jumped off the ramp and gave Alyson a hug, not caring what Peter thought of that. "Sure, as long as you stay off the lip, don't try anything fancy, and keep out of Peter's way," Jake said.

"Or," Peter joked as he executed a shuv-it — swinging the board around 180 degrees under his feet before stomping it down — "you could follow my tricks and we could be a synchronized skating team."

Alyson giggled, then turned back to Jake.

"You'll teach me, then?" she said, eyes bright with enthusiasm. Jake grinned. How could he resist that request? He wasn't very good at resisting anything Alyson asked, unless he considered it dangerous. He knew it wasn't normal to be both super-fond and ridiculously protective of his sister, but, well, that's just the way it had been since his dad had exited their lives.

Jake yanked Alyson's short brown braid before she could stop him and placed his skateboard on the bottom of the half-pipe. He stepped up and offered her a hand.

"Careful now."

Alyson shrugged off the hand and leapt up by herself, turning her back on Peter's show-off 360-flip to steady herself on Jake's board and look up expectantly at her brother.

"Okay, stand like this," Jake instructed.

Alyson did as she was told, but as Jake placed his hands on her slender shoulders and began to move her back and forth, he noticed her shift her right foot forward and move her left foot back.

"You're goofy," he exclaimed.

"Hey, don't be mean. I'm trying," Alyson protested.

"Sorry. Goofy doesn't mean stupid. It means you lead with your right foot," Jake replied. "It's fine. We just need to know. Keep rocking like that. You're doing okay," he encouraged as he lifted his hands from her shoulders. "Now bend your knees and put your arms out for balance. And Peter, will you stop shaking the whole structure? Take it a little easy while Alyson's learning, eh? You're not impressing her when she's concentrating on staying upright."

"Hey, if she can't handle a little shakin' and boogeyin', she'll never make it as —"

"Well, isn't this cute?" came a voice from the dirt path leading to the front of Sam's property. Jake, hands hovering over Alyson, turned to see four guys on BMX bikes. They looked perhaps a year older than Jake and Peter, and he'd seen them before, but wasn't sure which school they went to. Where had they come from, and how long had they been there? He shot a sideways glance at Peter, who stepped off his board and crossed his arms over his chest.

"What did you say?" Peter asked, his voice an octave deeper than normal.

"I said, how sweet," returned the lead BMXer in a jean jacket. "The half-pipe, I mean." Jake knew that's wasn't what he meant. "Mind if we try it out?"

Jake's eyes narrowed. "Sorry, but it's not strong or high enough for bikes. We just finished it and are trying it out ourselves. You from nearby?"

Jean-Jacket adjusted his bike helmet, scowled, and ignored the last question. "Not strong enough, you say? What, you built it from plans that came out of a cereal box or something?"

His eyes scanned Jake, Peter, and Alyson slowly, from top to bottom as he splayed long legs out from his bike.

Jake returned his hand to Alyson's shoulder, drew her closer to him. "Excuse me, but perhaps you're lost? This is private property and I don't believe we know you."

Jean-Jacket raised a dark eyebrow. One of his

buddies laughed, though Jake noticed another steal a quick glance behind him.

As Jake's pulse quickened, Peter spoke up. "Like my friend said, it's private property. Sorry our half-pipe isn't up to your standards."

None of the BMXers moved an inch. Jean-Jacket seemed to enjoy being engaged in a staring contest. Jake told himself to be careful and keep Peter in check with Alyson around.

"I'm just suggesting," Jean-Jacket finally said, dismounting from his bike and moving a step closer, "that you let us show you some real moves on that half-pipe — on bikes."

As Jake moved in front of Alyson, Peter jumped down from the half-pipe and sauntered over to one of Jean-Jacket's pals. "Hey, nice bikes." He placed his hands on one of the bikers' brake levers and snapped it twice. "So, where do you guys ride? I take it you're into half-pipe tricks — on something more impressive than this one, hey? Just cruising around, checking out the neighborhood? What do you think of the new skatepark in town?"

Jean-Jacket maneuvered his gaze from Jake to Peter.

"I think it should allow BMXs," he said slowly. "Do you know if it's going to?"

"Well, the new manager starts next Saturday, is

what we've heard. A former X Games vert champ. If he gives the word, we'll be seeing you around there, I guess. It'd be interesting to see your stuff. I'm Peter, by the way." He held his hand out to Jean-Jacket, bold as anything Jake had ever seen.

Jake held his breath for a count of three before Jean-Jacket grinned a toothy grin and cocked his head.

"Peter, eh? Judd." But he made no move to extend his hand or introduce his companions. "And you like BMXing. Sure you do. Well, too bad you don't think your little stack of wood here would hold us. But like you say, that skatepark opens next week. Maybe we'll catch you around there. Practice up, now."

Teeth flashing again, he moved back to his bike and hopped on it. Then the four bikers spun out of sight, leaving a cloud of dust.

Jake moved to shake Peter's hand. "Way to work it, buddy." Before Peter could reply, Sam's back door opened and three figures emerged, blinking in the bright sunlight.

Nancy and Sam made room for a tall, trim man with curly gray hair and a black, sleeveless shirt tucked into tailored white shorts. A silver chain around his neck glinted in the sun, echoed by the sparkle of a silver belt buckle inlaid with green stones. The man's amused green eyes fastened on Jake's half-pipe and the kids in turn. His eyes locked on Jake for so long Jake felt uncomfortable.

Nancy spoke. "Boys, and Alyson, this is Marco DeLisio, stunt coordinator and director of Excitement Films in Los Angeles, California. He's been doing stunt coordination for major filmmakers for many years. Now he's directing for the first time — on the action movie being shot here in Chilliwack. Marco, this is Jake and Peter, part-time summer staff at Sam's Adventure Tours, and Jake's sister, Alyson. Alyson's eleven, is that right?"

"Twelve," Alyson corrected her politely but firmly.

"Pleased to meet you," Marco said, hustling down the stairs and gripping each of their hands in turn, so firmly that Jake winced. "And you're skateboarders too?" His eyes returned to Jake as he said this.

"Yes, sir, and training hard for the stuntboy tryouts at the Chilliwack Xtreme Sk8park next week. Is that when they are, next week?" Peter's voice was way too gushy for Jake's liking.

Marco chuckled and turned to smile at Sam and Nancy. "Next Saturday it is. But do me some quick tricks now if you like. This looks like a sturdy ramp, by the way. Sam help you build it?"

"I built it," Jake said quietly.

"With no plans, in two days. Jake's a natural-born carpenter," Sam spoke up, prompting Jake's face to burn a little, especially as Marco turned his way again with The Stare.

"And athlete," Nancy added, winking at Jake. "He *and* Peter," she added hastily. "National-level white-water kayak racers, strong skiers and snowboarders, and accomplished downhill mountain bikers."

"But we've ditched all those for skateboarding," Peter piped up as he leapt to the deck and positioned his board to drop in.

Finally. He's looking at Peter now. Jake felt Alyson push him slightly toward the half-pipe, but he wasn't about to join Peter. Competing with Peter at this sport was tough enough without a movie director watching, and besides, it wasn't as if he was completely used to this half-pipe, or had time to think up what tricks he'd try. And why spoil Peter's show?

Of course, as Peter dropped down the transition and poured on speed, Jake realized his buddy wouldn't have even noticed another body on the half-pipe. He was in his element. As he rolled up the far side on a third pass, he bent his knees, reached down, and grabbed his deck as it cleared the far wall. Then he touched his front foot down on the top edge of the tranny and, back foot and opposite arm still holding the board high in mid-air, leapt back up to it, only to come flying back down onto the tranny, both feet back on the board.

Smooth as smooth, he rolled down the ramp and leaned forward to glide casually back to the opposite deck.

"Aha, a frontside boneless. Old school," Marco said. "How about some new school?"

Peter, face flushed with pleasure, pumped up again. Jake tugged on his baseball cap and scanned the faces of Peter's audience. Alyson's eyes shone with amazement, even though she'd seen Peter skate for years. Sam was shaking his head with a proud grin nearly as wide as his girth. Marco's face was a study of intense concentration, as if he were a human video camera.

Jake watched as Peter burst up over the lip and began to flip his deck. As it was turning, he grabbed it, then placed it back under his feet.

A kickflip Indy grab. Lean forward as you land or you'll have to bail like the last time I tried that, Jake thought.

Peter leaned forward and landed clean.

Okay, I could do that on a good day, Jake said to himself — without conviction.

Sweat trickled down Peter's face but failed to dim his glowing features as he bailed on his next trick and came to a smiling halt. Marco and Sam erupted into clapping. Alyson, Nancy, and Jake joined in politely.

"Bravo, son, not bad at all for a backyard half-pipe performance," Marco declared, moving down the steps to slap a hand on Peter's shoulder. "I dare say you'll have a blast at Xtreme Sk8's facilities. Must hurry to another meeting, but a pleasure meeting you kids." His gaze returned to Jake.

"Jake, right? I'll want to see you skate next time, okay?" Again, his gaze was long enough to make Jake squirm, as if the director were trying to remember Jake from somewhere. Then, "Sam, Nancy, looking forward to Monday's meeting." And he turned and strode down the path.

Sam galloped down the steps to walk at Marco's side out to the front. Jake pictured a limousine idling in front of Sam's Adventure Tours. Then he remembered seeing a little red convertible. Rich, for sure. And intense, no question. But who cared? He slipped an arm around Alyson's waist and climbed the stairs after Peter, who was — surprise, surprise — bantering 100 miles per hour to Nancy.

3   The Evans Family

Peter could hardly keep his feet on his bike pedals, he was so excited. He kept pulling wheelies, sprinting, and singing on the way back to Jake's. Only Jake's sluggish speed and long face were holding Peter back from reaching the Evans bungalow at a record-breaking rate. Even Alyson was riding faster than Jake, though she was being careful not to get too far ahead of him. Sometimes you'd think she was an older sister, the way she seemed to monitor Jake's moods.

Peter popped a wheelie again. An "in" with the director already, he mused, even *before* the official tryouts. Marco had been impressed with his performance for sure, even if he'd had to be careful not to show it. Peter figured he had a shot — surely he had a shot — at doing stunts for Marco's movie. And Marco seemed like a really nice guy. This could be his big break. He'd have to play it for everything he had.

Good thing Jake had finished the half-pipe; it would do for some training. But man, when that new skatepark was open, would Peter ever be in there. Dawn till dusk, if that's what it took. He was going to get a part in this movie no matter what it took. A springboard to his possible acting career. What a lucky break, a movie being shot in Chilliwack while he was visiting, and better yet, a sports one. He'd have been happy to be an extra in a big crowd scene, someone who ended up on the cutting room floor. But this, well, this was big. No way was he going to mess it up.

"Jake, old buddy, what's going on? Got a soft tire or something?"

Jake looked at him, sped up a little, but didn't reply. It wasn't like Jake not to be riding abreast or ahead. But come to think of it, Jake had been a little down all week, not his usual self at all. Never mind. Peter would help him buck up. He'd think of something they could do tonight.

"Hey, Alyson, you looked like a natural today," he called out as the three rode past a row of closed shops in a grungy part of town.

"Thanks," she tossed back with a smile that faded as fast as it had appeared. *Man, what was with her?* She was pretty enough when she smiled, but she seemed to be mimicking Jake's mopishness today. Maybe he'd take everyone out for ice cream tonight.

Jake's mom, too. She didn't get many breaks between her two jobs and keeping tabs on Jake and Alyson.

Peter braked as he spotted a man lying on the sidewalk. Hurt? Drunk? Napping?

"Hey there," he said, seeing the body stir. "You okay?" He glanced back to see that Jake and Alyson had stopped. But both were keeping their distance. Jake jerked his head as if to say "leave the guy alone." Peter bent closer. "I said are you okay?"

The man raised himself slowly on one elbow and smiled. His eyes were bloodshot, his hair matted. Peter noticed a sleeping bag behind him.

"Spare change?" the man mumbled.

"You bet." Peter dug in his pocket. He located a $5 bill and placed it in the man's grimy fingers. "Have a good day, sir," he said cheerfully as he hopped back on his bike and pedaled away.

"Hey, thanks!" the man called out.

Now Jake and Alyson came abreast.

"Peter, that was dumb. He'll just spend it on booze, you know," Jake declared.

"Maybe," Peter returned, "but he looked like he needed a meal to me."

"He stunk," Alyson said, nose crinkled.

"Of course he did. He doesn't have a home with a shower in it," Peter retorted. Seemed strange to him that Jake and Alyson, having been forced into money difficulties by their dad's disappearance, seemed indifferent to someone poorer than themselves.

"So, you never give money to down-and-outers?" Peter pressed Jake, curious.

"Even if I had any," Jake shot back, with a hint of sarcasm and bitterness that took Peter unawares, "I wouldn't. They give me the creeps."

"The creeps?" Peter watched Jake hang his head a little.

"Yup, no good reason. They just do."

"But I guess if we had a chocolate bar, we could give them that," Alyson piped up, as if trying to head off any tension between the guys.

"You're right, Alyson," Jake said in his older-brother tone.

Peter smiled. "What do you say we all go to the ice cream place tonight and get triple-decker sundaes, on me?"

"Alright!" Alyson shouted, preventing Jake from voicing whatever objection he seemed to be contemplating. He nodded and smiled.

So, thought Peter as they pulled up to Jake's house, *I can cheer them up.*

But as the three entered the kitchen, Peter saw Jake's mom place the phone on the receiver and turn puffy, reddened eyes away from them quickly. She slipped into her bedroom, from which she called out,

"Oh, hi kids. I'll be there in just a minute."

Peter shuffled his feet, avoiding Jake's and Alyson's eyes.

"Uh, I'm going to take a shower, okay? Then I'll help you with the barbecue, Jake."

Jake nodded, but he and Alyson didn't move from the doorway. Jake was resting his arm on Alyson's shoulder. Peter didn't know any other guys who were so tight with their sisters. In fact, he knew for a fact that Jake hadn't been like that before Mr. Evans had gone AWOL — "absent without leave," as they say in the army. Oh well, nice for them.

He showered, changed, and listened from behind Jake's bedroom door at the back of the one-storey house. Voices being kept deliberately too low to carry convinced him to stay in Jake's room, though he did catch the word "grandma." He dug into his pack, plucked out a book, and read till he dozed off in the afternoon heat.

"Memory tricks?!" a voice awakened him.

"Huh?"

"Memory tricks? You're reading a book on memory tricks? Thought all you read were skateboarding magazines," Jake said, flopping down on the bed opposite in their cramped room.

"Yeah, well, it's a good book," Peter said a little groggily. "Mom and Dad think I should try to get into a private school next year, and I have to study up for the entrance exam. Memorizing stuff helps. Anyway, I'm getting a kick out of the exercises in this book."

"Exercises?" Jake's tone was mildly teasing.

Peter sat up, grabbed his book, and thumbed through it. "Okay, let's say you have to remember a list of things in order. Here goes: Plant, banana, hotdog, chocolate. Know how you'd remember that list in order?"

"Not a clue, but sounds to me like you're hungry," Jake said, lifting his feet to rest on the bed's footboard and pulling his pillow under his head.

"You picture a house plant with a banana growing on it. You picture reaching over and breaking off the banana, and when you go to peel it, you find a hotdog instead of a banana inside it."

"Yuck."

"And when you go to bite into the hotdog, you find it's made of chocolate. Now, what's that list again?"

"Plant, banana, hotdog, chocolate."

"Okay, ready for a longer list?"

"Nope." Jake rearranged the pillow and crossed his feet. "Where is the private school, and why private school?"

"One close by our house in Seattle. Because my parents think it has better teachers and less fighting and drugs, I suppose. Who cares?"

"Well, I care," said Jake. "You may be the one doing memory tricks, but if my memory is correct, you'd fallen in with a couple of bad dudes who'd helped you develop a certain skill in shoplifting."

Peter groaned and covered his head with his pillow. Trust Jake to remember that. He'd been trying to forget it. "Yeah, you're right. Mom and Dad never found out about that, but they knew those guys weren't — well, they just knew. You know the way parents are?"

He saw Jake make a slight grimace and then smile. "Yeah, I know. So they're going to send you off to a private school so you won't get into any more trouble. I'm glad. It'll be good for you. Now, what were you saying about memories?"

Peter was glad Jake had changed the subject. "Guess what percentage of our brains we use in a whole lifetime?"

"Now we're going from memory tricks to brain trivia?"

"Sure; they're connected, duh. And the answer is less than five percent. Bet you also didn't know that humans have ten billion brain cells. But here's what's important: Kids who don't use global learning remember only three percent of stuff from school classes. The memory trick I just taught you is part of global learning." He knew he was pushing it, but it was kind of fun to yank Jake's chain. A little payback for bringing up the shoplifting thing.

"I don't know about global learning," said Jake, springing up off the bed, "but how about some global warming of those burgers you said you'd help me barbecue? And I think you also mentioned taking us all out for ice cream afterwards. Now that's the first really brainy thing you've said all day."

"Absolutely," Peter agreed, slamming his book shut.

An hour later, Peter felt proud to tote dishes of ice cream from the counter to the booth of the ice-cream shop where the Evanses had seated themselves.

"Extra pineapple bits on it, just like you ordered, Mrs. Evans," he said.

"Peter, please. You keep forgetting I've told you to call me Sandra."

"Uh-huh, sorry." He was relieved she'd pulled herself together and was looking more relaxed than earlier that afternoon, but he couldn't help reflecting on how different she looked than a few years ago, when he'd lived next door. She was skin and bones now, sadder, and never wore makeup anymore. She seemed tired all the time, and her occasional moments of cheerfulness often struck him as forced. She also wasn't as strict with Jake and Alyson as she used to be, Peter mused. Of course, that might be useful one of these evenings if he could convince Jake to sneak out and find some fun around town.

"So, what's your plan tomorrow? It's your day off at Sam's, right?" Sandra asked as she sat with her spoon poised over her sundae. Peter realized he'd been staring at her.

"Skatepark," Peter and Jake declared together.

"Is it finished and open?" Sandra crossed long legs and dangled a worn sandal off one toe. Peter reflected that his mother never wore sandals without some exotic shade of toenail polish. He really didn't mind Mrs. Evans's — no, Sandra's — relaxed earthiness, though.

"Are there going to be lessons for beginners there?" Alyson asked.

"It's going to open any day, they keep saying," Peter said. "And you don't need lessons, Alyson. You have a teacher."

Sandra looked at Jake, then at Alyson. "It's not enough that Jake does all these crazy sports. You have to take one up, too?" she addressed Alyson.

"Don't worry, Mom. Jake and Peter won't let me get hurt."

"Uh-huh. I know all about Jake and Peter's safety record," Sandra teased back. "Just don't any of you show up in the emergency room on my shift. Wear your helmets and pads."

Peter and Jake nodded obediently, resisting the urge to exchange a look. Helmets and pads were for nerds. They wouldn't be caught dead wearing them unless they had to, and if Alyson wanted lessons, she'd better not say a thing. But Peter reflected on how Sandra's night job as a nurse's aide at the hospital probably exposed her to some ugly injuries. Like Jake, she could find any excuse to worry.

"Well, I'm off now," Sandra said, reaching over to squeeze Alyson's hand and tussle Jake's hair. She stood up. "I must get ready for work. Thanks for the ice cream, Peter. You're a real gentleman."

This sent up peels of laughter from Jake and Alyson, but Peter didn't mind. Anything that made the Evanses laugh lately was a difficult feat accomplished he decided, as he savored an extra-large spoonful of marshmallow-caramel sundae covered in chopped pecans.

4   A Skating Shrink

Jake wasn't sure which he noticed first: the rusted Mustang with steam flowing from its engine in the otherwise empty parking lot of the skatepark, or the figure bent over that engine.

"Hold up," he told Peter as he stepped off his skateboard to peer at the raised hood of the car.

"Need any help?" he addressed the muscular body of a young man. That prompted a head to jerk up. A head with dreadlocks, and a mouth holding a wrench.

"I do if you know anything about engines," said a smiling black man of about twenty-five.

"Try me," Jake said, ignoring Peter's impatient look. "My dad used to own a Mustang. Same year, I think."

"Really? Right on!"

The fellow stood up, wiped his greasy hands on a rag, and pointed underneath the hood. "It started smelling and smoking, and then stopped on me."

Jake tried not to smile. "Did you notice the temperature gauge before it went out?"

"It was right off the clock. And when I opened the hood, it was like a geyser in there."

Jake peered around the plume of steam and borrowed the man's rag to inspect the fan belt. "I'd say your fan belt isn't tight enough. The fan isn't turning fast enough to keep the engine cool, so your rad has boiled over."

"Hmmm, guess I should have been able to figure that out myself," the man said a little sheepishly. "So what now?"

Jake looked into the back seat. "Can we use those jugs of water you've got in your car? And your wrench, once that engine has cooled a bit?"

"You certainly can. You be the man!"

Jake grinned. Peter slumped down to sit on his skateboard.

"While we're waiting, might as well introduce ourselves," the man said, extending his hand. "I'm Kwasi Kumar."

Jake nodded and shook his hand, taking in his muscular build, baggy shorts, sleeveless T, and huge shoes. "I'm Jake."

"I'm Peter," Peter spoke up. "What kind of name is Kwasi?"

"Afro-Caribbean," Kwasi said, "though I was born

and raised in Toronto. Moved to Chilliwack two weeks ago. Came here to run this skatepark starting this week." He grinned and eyed each of their skateboards in turn, the beads from his dreadlocks bouncing as he did.

"You're the new manager of the skatepark?" Jake said, looking the man up and down again. "Is it true you were in the X Games?"

"Silver medallist eight years ago," he said, cracking a wide grin. "Now I'm just a starving school dropout. I'm taking a year off graduate school to earn money and take night classes to get my grades up. Nearly flunked out for doing more skateboarding than studying. Thought I'd do a voluntary time-out before they gave me the boot."

"Studying *and* running a skatepark? Sounds like a lot of work," Peter said.

"Yup. I'm studying to be a psychologist. Takes at least four years beyond college to be a qualified shrink, and I've got one year to go," Kwasi said, still grinning with what struck Jake as a 1,000-watt smile. The man radiated energy. Jake couldn't help but like him. And somehow, it wasn't hard to imagine him pulling off crazy stunts on a skateboard.

Jake rose and gently removed the radiator cap, fetched the water jugs from Kwasi's back seat, and slowly poured water into the radiator. Aware that the two were watching him, he squared his shoulders, replaced the radiator cap, then took the wrench firmly in hand to loosen the fan belt adjuster and get the belt snug on the last position possible. He tightened the bolt, stood back, and looked at Kwasi, who was watching him with wide eyes.

"Try it now," Jake suggested.

Kwasi hopped into the driver's seat and turned the key in the ignition. As the engine roared to life, Jake redirected his eyes to the rear of the car.

"Right on! Far out!" Kwasi said.

Jake smiled. "Better get that muffler fixed before you get pulled over," he suggested. "So, when will the skatepark open? We were just headed over there to find out ourselves."

Kwasi lowered the hood of his car, grabbed a chain hanging from his belt, and yanked a heavily loaded key ring from his shorts pocket. "It could open right now, if you like."

"Yes!" Jake and Peter exclaimed.

Kwasi's ancient Mustang, breaking any city noise regulations, roared one last time before Kwasi cut the engine. Meanwhile, Jake and Peter's foot-propelled skateboards made their way across the lot and around the building to the front doors. As they drew near the entryway, Jake slowed. The three toughs who seemed to have staked out the plaza in front of the skatepark were hard at it. A tall, sinewy boy in a black knit cap from which tufts of brown hair stuck out was skating really well. Though they'd observed him before, it was hard not to stare. His sure, swift moves made him look like someone who could turn pro with very little polishing. Like on the other two occasions they'd seen him, Jake wondered if he was sponsored. He was dressed neck to soles in black, save for a fancy logo on his T-shirt. He was fifteen, and Jake knew which school he attended.

"That guy looks like he was born on a skateboard," Jake said to Peter, voice low.

Peter shifted from one foot to another. "We'll see," he said.

Jake turned to watch the boy nearest the black-clad hotshot. As short as he was quick, the Chinese-Canadian boy with chains around his neck was pulling tricks in rapid-fire succession. Though his abilities ranked closer to Jake's than Peter's, he had a certain flash to his tricks that, together with an ever-present grin, broadcast full exuberance for the sport. As Kwasi slammed his car door and headed toward Jake and Peter, Jake eyed the third boy. Something about this shirtless, skinny boy with the grim face made Jake uneasy. His tricks were slow but deliberate, competent but low-key, as if he'd resigned himself to a role as backdrop to his buddies.

"So, welcome to Xtreme Sk8," Kwasi said, eyes shining with pride. "The sixth largest private skatepark in North America, with every obstacle known to skater-kind. No expense spared, thanks to a fanatic investor. It's my job to keep it safe, fun, and filled."

He paused and followed Jake's and Peter's eyes to the trio of skaters, who finished off some tricks, stepped off their boards, and moved toward Kwasi.

"Hey, Aaron," Kwasi called out to the boy in the black hat, moving forward to hold his fist out for a "pound." "Smooth moves there." Aaron nodded, completed the high-five, but directed most of his energy to glaring at Jake and Peter.

"Bruce!" Kwasi continued, slapping the Chinese-Canadian boy on the back. "Hang any higher on those moves and those chains are going to fall off." This drew a smirk on Bruce's face, but he was clearly distracted by Jake and Peter being with Kwasi. He and Aaron had been pretty quick to drive Jake and Peter off on both their previous encounters. That is, neither Jake nor Peter had considered it worth a fistfight to share the little plaza.

Kwasi's pretty down with these guys, Jake thought uneasily.

Finally, Kwasi nodded at the shirtless boy, whose eyes shifted everywhere but on Kwasi's face.

"Gabe," he said quietly. "Good to see you." He made no move to approach Gabe, who hung at the fringes of the group, didn't reply, and began fiddling with a coin he'd pulled from his worn shorts pocket.

"So, Aaron, Bruce, Gabe — meet my new friends Jake and Peter. They're as stoked to see inside our building as you were last week. Join us for the tour?"

Bruce and Gabe looked briefly at Aaron, who nodded so slightly that Jake nearly missed it. No question who was leader of the three, he reflected. The first letter of Aaron's name was also the first letter in the word "alpha," another word for leader, he mused. Bruce looked like he could be friendly in some circumstances. B for "beta," a follower, Jake decided, pleased with the fun he was having. And Gabe? Jake was inwardly grinning now. Gaunt, grim, gruff, or glowering. Certainly not gracious or genial.

The group of six moved forward in uneasy formation, all but Kwasi gripping skateboards, as the manager bombarded them with details of the park's final construction process. As they reached the double steel doors, Kwasi pulled out his chain full of keys once again, and before Jake and Peter could draw a breath, the group was inside a bewildering wonderland of constructions.

"Whoa," was all Jake could think. Bigger than two pro basketball courts combined, it was divided neatly into two sections for street and tranny skating. Kwasi was right. Not a single element was missing. Hubbas (downward-sloping ledges), funboxes (boxes with ramps on each side), handrails, ledges of every description, hips (where two ramps meet and change direction), and banks (moveable ramps). Even a Euro-gap and pyramid. And that was just the street stuff. The tranny area featured both wooden and concrete bowls, mini ramps (half-pipes less than six feet tall), spines (where two ramps meet), and, most impressive of all, a ramp that had to be twelve feet high — two full feet of vert.

"The park is 12,000 square feet altogether," Kwasi was saying as he flicked on some lights, "and caters to both old and new school. Old is coming back in a big way," he informed his tour group, prompting Aaron and Bruce to sneer meaningfully at each other behind Kwasi's back.

Guess they don't agree with that, Jake thought.

"And it's finally opening after five months of construction," Peter said, breaking the silence among the boys. "What did this set someone back, Kwasi, if you're allowed to say?"

"Aha, you're not shy, are you?" Kwasi observed jovially. "Who wants to guess?"

"Quarter of a million," Aaron said without hesitation. Obviously the leader.

"Nah, more," Bruce guessed. His handsome Asian

face revealed a quick mind when lit up like it was at the moment, Jake thought. And maybe a business savvy the others lacked.

"Four hundred thou," Peter contributed.

"Getting warmer," Kwasi said conspiratorially. "Try half a million."

Bruce whistled. "No one's ever going to get that back. This is Chilliwack, not New York City."

Kwasi shrugged and rested a hand on Bruce's shoulder. Bruce seemed not to even notice. If Kwasi had moved to Chilliwack only two weeks ago, how did he know these guys so well? Jake wondered. Obviously, he'd been dropping in a lot before his official start date and had made a point of befriending this group.

"Bruce, we're going to get R.O.I., no worries," Kwasi declared.

"R.O.I.?" Aaron spoke up as if annoyed at Kwasi sharing a special language with Bruce.

"Return on investment, Aaron," Kwasi said. "Payback. Excitement Films' gig will help with that." He turned to Jake and Peter. "You boys know about the movie being shot here?"

Jake hoped Peter wouldn't jump in and shoot his mouth off, but he shouldn't have wasted the thought.

"Yes, we know Marco," Peter said, drawing himself up a little. "He's hired our employer, Sam Miller, for some stunt coordination."

"Really? You work for Sam's Adventure Tours? Right on. So, Jake and Peter, Aaron, Bruce, and Gabe here have been dying to initiate this park, and today's the first day the construction crews have been gone. There's a little post-construction cleanup still to do, but if the five of you help me with that, I say the whole facility is yours for the afternoon. We open officially in two days: on Tuesday."

"We're in," Peter spoke up.

"What needs doing, Kwasi?" Aaron asked, pushing a little ahead of Peter.

"Tunes!" Bruce exclaimed. "Let's get the sound system happening and we'll do whatever you say, boss. Can I choose the station or CDs?"

Kwasi laughed and produced another key to the office, where he spent some time explaining buttons and knobs to Bruce, while Gabe, the sullen one — who, like Jake, had not spoken a word yet — hung near them, listening intently.

Soon hip-hop music was blaring at a decibel level that shook sawdust from the rafters. Before they knew it, Jake and Peter were absorbed in sweeping, hauling construction debris outside, and peeling protective plastic from some of the ramps. They worked closely together, avoiding the other boys, who gave them a wide berth as well. Kwasi, all the while, directed the operation like a cross between a traffic controller and coach. Everyone seemed eager to please him, even the ever-grim Gabe. And Kwasi never missed an opportunity to encourage each member of the team.

"Jake and Peter, you guys are hard workers. No wonder Sam has snatched you up. Now you can countersink all the top sheets, screw them down, paint the sides and rails, and sweep and mop the ramps — in that order, please." Jake wondered how they were going to remember all that, but Peter lit up.

"Hey, Jake, there's a good use for global learning. Visualize a bed sheet hanging from your mom's clothesline with pictures of screws all over it. Then imagine…"

Jake rolled his eyes, but Kwasi, who'd overheard, said, "You know, Peter, global learning is useful for remembering a run of tricks at skate competitions, too. I'm doing my thesis on how memory works. I'll buy you a soda sometime and we'll have a discussion on memory tricks."

"Cool!" Peter said, giving Jake a "told-you-it-was-interesting" look.

At noon, just as Kwasi seemed to be running out of things to assign the boys, there was a knock at the front doors.

"Bruce, check it out, okay?" Kwasi ordered.

Bruce opened the door and turned to Kwasi with

astonishment. "It's two extra-large pizzas being delivered. Did you do that, Kwasi?"

Kwasi chuckled, produced his wallet, and ambled over to pay the pizza delivery boy, whose eyes were darting around the complex in awe. As Kwasi tipped him, the boy's eyes went even wider.

"Thanks!"

"You're welcome. And if you're a skater, we open on Tuesday. As for the rest of you, can't skate on empty stomachs. So eat up. I'm off to turn Bruce's music down a notch and do some paperwork in the office."

"Oh, one more thing." He swiveled around and surveyed the boys sternly. "To skate in here, you have to wear a helmet at all times, and pads in the tranny area — in other words, on the half-pipe. For today, you can borrow some from that pile over there."

"No way!" Aaron protested.

"You mean the inexperienced kids, right?" Peter asked.

But Jake could see Kwasi's face was deadly serious.

"No exceptions," Kwasi said, waiting to head to the office until everyone had mumbled "yes."

Jake had no idea how famished he was till he dove into the pizza. As he and Peter ate, perched on a skate ledge across from the three whispering boys, he kept wondering how this afternoon was going to play out. He hoped Kwasi wasn't planning on straying too far, and that the boys might relax and talk to Peter and him. He needn't have bothered with the last thought.

5 Stoked

Aaron made the first move. Leaving Bruce and Gabe to finish off their pizza, he stood, exchanged his black knit hat for a helmet from the box of jumbled equipment near the office, and strode to the wooden bowl as if his name had just been announced on Kwasi's public-announcement system. His back to Jake and Peter, he stepped onto his board and began rolling, roaming the entire facility like a restless fair attendee deciding which ride to take first. Here and there he clipped the edge of a hip, or executed a lazy kickturn. Soon he poured on speed, landed some ollies, and began linking one trick after another. He made it all look so effortless, Jake thought. The minute Aaron pulled his first air seemed to work like a signal for Peter and Bruce, who leapt up, grabbed helmets from the equipment box, and began kicking up their own racket on the setup.

Aaron appeared as unaware of their entry onto his stage as a theater star would be of stagehands. But Peter wasn't going for much of a warm-up this afternoon. He gunned his board for a series of moves, which Aaron acknowledged with a glance from the corner of his eye. As Bruce started whipping up a flurry of action in a corner of the street section, Peter glided over to the giant vertical ramp.

Jake glanced at Gabe, who seemed lost in his own fog beside the empty pizza box. Time to hit it up, Jake decided as he stood, ambled over to the helmet box, made his own selection, and positioned himself on his board. At first, Jake was happy to wander the enormous floor like an explorer, pulling some moves as passing features seemed to suggest them. Nothing crazy: just good, solid stuff. He could feel his legs getting into the rhythm, taking on curves and humps with growing confidence. He noticed Bruce swaying and jumping to the tunes, his body and wheels invisibly leashed to the aggressive beat. Music was clearly Bruce's inspiration. As the board flowed beneath him, Bruce appeared oblivious to the undeclared competition heating up between Aaron and Peter, or of Jake cruising the floor like an excited tourist, or of Gabe finally joining the action, grinding every rail in the place as if he were in charge of wearing them down before opening day. Jake had to give Gabe credit: He flew on and off the rails with perfect precision.

It wasn't all flow for any of them, of course. There was lots of bailing, but that was just part of skating. Jake was feeling good. This place was awesome. He settled into the street section and started working on rolling down the pyramids and grinding some ledges. Yes! One after another, he was landing tricks, driving higher and faster. Throwing away his usual caution, egged on perhaps by Aaron and Peter's bowl action, he went for a bluntslide, ollieing up onto a ledge, then pushing down on his tail and leaning into a long slide before popping off.

As he landed it with barely a waver, he saw both Aaron and Peter glance his way.

And why shouldn't they? he thought. Hadn't Peter said he was way better than he usually gave himself credit for? He just had to go for it, had to feel when his body was into pushing its limits. For a good hour, the boys hammered away at the sport's catalog of tricks. Occasionally someone would bail or curse, and once or twice, someone had to veer quickly to avoid crashing into someone else. Mostly, however, each skater was absorbed in his own thing, even if Aaron and Peter were clearly playing off each other. Harmless one-upping, Jake thought, until he saw Aaron motor six feet above the vert ramp's deck and pull a nice heelflip. (He flipped the board with his heel.)

Peter, don't you dare, Jake thought, slowing his own board to a near standstill. Like a movie suddenly thrust into slow motion, the scene took on a new tempo. Gabe and Bruce, like Jake, had paused as if someone had declared intermission. Aaron was poised on the deck of the vert ramp, feigning impatience for Peter to move so he could drop in, when really he wasn't going to miss Peter's next trick for anything in the world. Jake bit his tongue as he saw Peter drop in. He bit it harder as Peter set up and duplicated Aaron's last trick to perfection. For a split second, Jake imagined the two as fighter pilots performing difficult maneuvers in the sky, leaving zigzagging streams of vapor for observers far below to admire.

"Right on, Peter!" Kwasi's voice suddenly boomed over the loudspeaker. Jake guessed that Kwasi had just looked up and had missed Aaron's move. Aaron turned dark eyes toward the office, then back on Jake, catching him in the act of staring.

"So, what do you think?" Kwasi's enthusiasm poured through the office mike as he switched off the music. "Thanks for being my front team. I'm guessing you're all having a good time and approve of our new park?"

Aaron nodded and gave Kwasi a thumbs up, then leaned down to pick up his board. As the boy straightened up, Jake noticed that he looked startled to find Peter beside him.

"Nice skating," Peter said in a lower-than-usual voice.

Aaron hesitated, but only for a split second. Then, with slightly narrowed eyes, he nodded.

"Rad park," he replied. "Check you later."

Jake watched Gabe follow Aaron toward the door. Bruce hung his head and sighed as if disappointed that his buddies were leaving so soon. But he picked up his board.

"Hey," he addressed Jake and Peter with what seemed to Jake a genuine smile. "Sick place. Later."

"Off already? See you next sesh, bro," Kwasi shouted as he emerged from his office. Jake knew "sesh" was skate talk for "session."

Kwasi wandered over to Jake and Peter. "So, you were killing it," he complimented them. "Either of you planning to show for Marco's tryouts on Saturday? I'm sure he'd like to see your stuff."

"I am, and Jake had better be," Peter declared, elbowing Jake as if Jake couldn't speak for himself.

As Kwasi turned to study Jake for a moment, his eyes reminded Jake of Nancy's: instantly penetrating. Great. Just what Jake needed, another mind reader trying to figure him out. Then Kwasi winked and turned. "Thanks again for the car repair, Jake. And we'll see you boys tomorrow if you want one last sesh before the doors open to the public."

"Thanks, but we're at Sam's tomorrow," Jake said.

"Well, I'm here seven to seven," he informed them, "whether the doors are open or not. Just knock loudly."

With that, he strolled back to the office whistling. Jake, heading toward the door with Peter, heard the sound system click back on. As reggae music filled the empty skatepark, Jake glanced back and smiled. Kwasi was grooving to the music like a lead singer in a band, elbows gently air drumming, body swaying, hair flying. Jake wondered what routine Bruce would dream up to skate to that.

When the alarm went off the next morning, Monday, Jake rolled over and stared bleary-eyed at the clock and Peter's empty bed. "Who's been messing with my clock?" he asked. "I set it for eight, not six thirty."

"Yeah, but Kwasi's open at seven. That gives us two hours' skating before we have to be at Sam's," Peter said as he pulled on a T-shirt. "I'll make breakfast if you promise to be quiet."

Jake shook his head, half amazed and half amused at Peter's keenness.

"Did you ask me if I wanted to skateboard at seven in the morning?"

"Nope. I just knew you did, with tryouts coming up and all."

Jake stifled a grin, forced himself out of bed, dressed, tiptoed into the kitchen, and accepted peanut butter smeared on a bagel from Peter.

"You've been up since six preparing this breakfast, I presume?" Jake whispered.

"Shhh," was Peter's response. They exited the house with boards on their backpacks and biked the short distance to Xtreme Sk8 without seeing a single car on the road.

Jake's watch read ten minutes to seven as they rapped on the double steel doors.

"Crazy not here," a nasal voice behind them declared.

Jake and Peter whirled around to see a tall man of about thirty with a scarred face and fingers curled into an unnatural position on both hands. The man blinked groggily in the morning light, his eyes unfocused. Jake noted the cowboy boots, cowboy hat. A belt buckle depicting a bucking bronco held the man's jeans on his strong-built frame. A drunk? A bum? Jake's knee-jerk reaction was to step back. But the man didn't look dangerous or reek like a street person. His clothes were clean, and he even smelled of cheap cologne. The man unfurled one hand to tug on his cowboy hat as if that would give him greater authority.

"Crazy not here yet," he repeated louder, then erupted into an entirely unexpected giggle.

Okay, Jake was catching on. The guy was a kook, a retard, what you're supposed to call "mentally challenged." He didn't look threatening, but Jake's feet took another few steps back anyway. He willed Peter to come away.

"You mean Kwasi?" Peter was saying. He pulled a granola bar out of his shorts pocket and offered it to the man.

"No, thanks. Not hungry," the man returned, drawing himself up to his full, towering height and studying Peter with the open stare of a young child.

"Ah, you've met Lex," Kwasi said as he approached from behind. "Lex, this is Jake and Peter. They're skaters. Jake and Peter, this is Lex, a rehab patient working for Xtreme Sk8. I see you're in for some early morning training? Right on!"

Lex echoed "right on!" and looked pleased with himself.

Jake stole a look at Peter, who was chewing thoughtfully on the bar that Lex had turned down.

"So, what exactly does Lex do for Sk8?" Peter asked as Kwasi began fingering his key ring for the front door key.

"Lex here will be mopping the ramps, doing daily screw checks underneath all the obstacles, and cleaning the wheel marks and loogies off the wall."

"Loogies?"

"Spit, my dear Peter. You *are* a gentleman to not know that."

This sent Lex into another giggling fit, which Jake considered rather appropriate.

"Lex used to work rodeos and suffered a brain injury when a bull threw him against the stands two years ago. I'm working with Vancouver's Brain Trauma Therapy Centre to help rehabilitate their graduates to the workforce, where possible."

"Their *graduates*? Hmmm. Good stuff," Peter said as he finished his bar, parked his bike just inside the door, dropped his board to the floor, and raced off to the vert ramp.

"If you need anything, Jake, just ask Lex or myself," Kwasi said, his eyes momentarily penetrating Jake's efforts to hide his discomfort with Lex.

"Yeah, thanks," Jake mumbled as he removed his backpack and prepared to join Peter. Why should he care if Kwasi had hired a "rehab patient" to mop the skatepark? Kwasi was a shrink, after all. Or three-quarters of one, anyway.

He and Peter skated for an hour and a half on their own. This time, the session felt relaxed. No pressure from Aaron's crew, and the hubbas and ledges felt more familiar to him today. Once again, he could feel his confidence soar, propelling him to take chances. And since Peter was doing more sensible stuff on both the street and tranny sections, Jake was matching him consistently in speed, style, and level of challenge. In fact, after a while, Jake could tell that this was eating at Peter.

"Jake, you're destroying the place," Peter said. "Looking clean, old buddy." But he upped the ante with a switch three-flip (flipping his board both vertically and horizontally while switching stance) as he said it, knowing Jake had never done one before.

Jake took the bait. Peter was the most competitive person he knew, and it was fun to rile him a little. As for the second most competitive person he knew — *that would be me,* Jake thought with a smile as he inward heel-flipped to manual (flipped the board both vertically and horizontally, then did the skater's equivalent of a wheelie, balancing on two wheels).

Peter stared at Jake. "You're pumped, Jake, aren't you? I'd better watch my ass." Then he grinned and checked his watch.

"Sam time."

The two stepped down from the deck and paused to wave at Kwasi and Lex in the office, when they noticed a figure leaning against the wall near the front doorway.

"Marco, good morning," Peter said. "Didn't expect to see you here."

"Nor I you," Marco returned, but he was looking at Jake, not Peter.

Would you please stop staring at me, Jake thought. The guy was weird, for sure. But he'd probably seen Jake pull off the inward heel manual. That pleased Jake, somehow. Would Jake have managed it if he'd known Marco was watching? Probably not, but that didn't matter now.

"Good morning," Jake addressed Marco politely. "Kwasi and Lex are in the office. We've gotta get to Sam's."

"Bye," Marco said, nodding and ambling toward the office. "See you boys Saturday, then. *Both* of you, right?"

"You're wanted," Peter kidded Jake out of Marco's earshot.

"Yeah, like at Sam's five minutes ago," Jake responded. "How fast can *you* bike?"

6   Right On!

It was Friday, the day before tryouts, and that's all it seemed Peter could talk about. Tryouts, the skatepark — open since Tuesday to the public — and Kwasi, who'd been coaching them whenever they showed up at Xtreme Sk8.

"The problem with Kwasi," Peter was saying as the boys hauled themselves out of bed, "is that he never goes off-duty as a shrink."

This made Jake pause from rooting around his drawer for a sock that didn't have a hole in it. "Such as?" he prompted Peter, welcoming a story. Today was a half-day at Sam's, he reminded himself, which gave them the morning off.

"Well, we happened to be standing across the room when we saw Gabe do the little kids' science trick of pouring baking powder and vinegar into Lex's cleaning bucket to make it suddenly foam over the top, which upset Lex and made everyone else laugh. All Kwasi says to me is, 'Gabe comes from a dysfunctional family. He's got social issues.'"

"That's rich. Gabe is the definition of *anti*-social."

"Yeah, and then he hears Aaron and Bruce calling Lex 'Cowboy' and trying to get him to do stuff that isn't his job. I was expecting him to go over and ream them out, but he just tells me, 'Aaron and Bruce are helping Lex feel useful. Lex thrives on any interaction with you skaters, and he can take care of himself.'"

"He can until they punch him out," Jake speculated.

"I actually said that to Kwasi, and you know what he said? 'If Aaron and Bruce get physical with Lex, it's Aaron and Bruce I'd be worried about.' Then he started bugging me about you."

"Like how?"

"Like, 'What gives with Jake being so withdrawn? Is there something going on in his life right now that I should know about?'"

"You told him to back off and stick to rehab patients, I hope?" Jake was finished dressing and figuring they should head to the kitchen for breakfast.

"No, I told him that Saturday was your dad's birthday, that your dad disappeared three years ago to that day, and that your mom was making you and Alyson acknowledge his birthday by going to supper with your grandma — your dad's mom."

Jake stood stock-still. Shock and anger rose like mercury on a thermometer plunged into boiling water. "And just where did you get that information, and what right…"

"Alyson told me. She told me because you hadn't. She obviously thought that I, as your best friend, should know something like that. It might have helped me handle your moodiness lately, Jake. And since Kwasi has become our coach, I saw no harm in giving him what he was halfway to figuring out anyway. He's been talking to Sam, you know. He'd have gotten what he wanted from Sam if not from me."

With every word, Peter's face was growing redder, and his defiant tone was fading. Jake could tell that Peter knew he'd crossed a line, no matter how he was trying to justify things. Jake felt himself shake with anger and humiliation. Coaches don't need to know intimate details of people's lives, and no way had Jake adopted Kwasi as his coach. How could Jake face Kwasi this morning, knowing he had that information? How dare Alyson tell Peter, and how *dare* Peter tell Kwasi.

But Jake pressed his fingernails into his palms and breathed out very, very slowly. He didn't want a row with Peter right now. He had a right to be furious with Peter, but he didn't want to shout. Not when Peter was leaving this morning for two days at a fancy hotel with his parents. They'd phoned him last evening, and the minute Peter had told them about Saturday's stuntboy tryouts, they'd insisted on driving up immediately and staying in Chilliwack right through the event. Jake could picture them in the stands that Lex had begun erecting yesterday, holding hands and never taking their eyes off their precious only son. And who would Jake have rooting for him? Alyson. And his mother, briefly, if her day-job employer allowed her a long lunch break. Which was great, of course. But it was times like this that Jake felt the loss of his dad so keenly he could not believe it had been three years since he'd disappeared.

The pain of not having a caring dad in the stands was one thing. The bitter irony of the tryouts being on his dad's birthday, the day that always made him want to curl up in a deep hole alone, was too depressing to contemplate. No coach or amateur shrink could help Jake navigate his way through that.

"Jake," Peter was saying. "Jake, I'm sorry. Really sorry."

Peter apologizing was unheard of. He *really* knew he'd blown it. Jake softened as he realized he'd been giving Peter the silent treatment for a couple of minutes while lost in his own thoughts.

"Can we not talk about it?" Jake asked.

"Okay, but Jake?"

"What?"

"Alyson begged me to remind you that you promised

her a skateboard lesson at the new skatepark this morning. You forgot both Wednesday and yesterday after Sam's. She said she waited for you there for an hour both times. I'd have said something when we left Sam's if I'd known you'd set that up."

Jake's head and shoulders drooped. He'd let Alyson down. Twice, even. How could he? Maybe that's why she'd told Peter what was up with Saturday. Well, there was no choice now. He'd have to show at the skatepark this morning. But he'd avoid Kwasi.

Jake and Alyson set off for the skatepark as soon as Peter and his parents had pulled out of Jake's driveway in their silver BMW. Nice for him that he gets some time with them, Jake thought, waving at Richard and Laura Montpetit and trying to be positive. But it was going to make life bleak today and tomorrow.

"Jake, Peter told me they have lots of cool stuff at the skatepark. Think there will be anything easy enough for me?"

"Sure, Alyson. We'll just stake out our own corner and have you doing some tricks in no time."

"Jake, have you ever ridden a BMX?"

"Nope."

"They can do impressive moves on a half-pipe too, you know."

"Of course I know."

"They should be allowed at the new skatepark."

"Maybe. That's up to Kwasi."

"He said no."

"How would you know that?"

"I just heard." She sounded stubbornly evasive. Jake smiled. His sister was definitely becoming a teenager, declaring her independence from him slowly but surely. But she'd still chosen him for skateboard lessons, and hopefully would be his best cheerleader at tryouts tomorrow. *If* he was up to going.

When they arrived at the skatepark, they found the doors ajar and the railing fanatic—that is, Gabe—hard at it. Lex was scrubbing the walls around the tranny section, his cowboy hat bobbing with the motion.

"Is that the crazy cowboy?" Alyson whispered, pointing to Lex.

"Don't point. Yes, that's him," Jake responded. Jake nodded at Gabe, shirtless as always, his ribs all but sticking out through his skin. Jake noticed an ugly bruise on Gabe's cheek and another down one side of his chest. Although most efforts to talk to Gabe had been a waste of time, Jake decided to try again, especially since Aaron and Bruce weren't around.

"Hi, Gabe. This is my sister, Alyson. She's just learning. Looks like you had a gnarly bail?"

Gabe looked up and met Jake's eyes, which was something for Gabe. He shook his head yes, then looked quickly away.

Jake, feeling emboldened by Gabe's acknowledgement, said, "Hope Kwasi gave you some ice for that. Must've hurt."

To his surprise, Gabe returned an entire sentence: "I'm always banging myself up."

"Funny, 'cause I've never seen you slam once," Jake remarked, amazed that they were having a real conversation. But the compliment seemed to shut Gabe down fast. The boy stomped on his tail, clenched his board in his hand, and walked away so abruptly that Jake was left feeling foolish.

Alyson, probably knowing her voice might carry, wisely said nothing. Gabe plunked himself down in the empty office and inserted a grunge CD, prompting Lex to put his hands over his ears and frown. Jake concentrated on working with Alyson. He nodded to Kwasi when the manager strode in with a steaming cup of coffee in hand.

"Kwasi, this is my sister, Alyson."

"Right on! Welcome!" Kwasi said but didn't linger.

Jake also introduced Alyson to Aaron and Bruce when they arrived. Aaron looked Alyson up and down dismissively and asked, "Peter taking the day off?"

"The morning, anyway," Jake said without elaboration.

Aaron's face reflected a hint of a smile as he sped off to his usual turf, the bowls. After Jake had worked with Alyson for an hour, he walked her the four blocks to her babysitter's as planned.

"Why can't I just stay with you at the skatepark till you go to Sam's?"

"'Cause Mom had this arranged."

"I'm too old to need a babysitter, you know."

"I know."

"Well, then tell Mom."

"I have." He smiled and hugged Alyson, then waved as he turned back toward Xtreme Sk8.

It was nice not to have to show up at Sam's till noon. He'd decided to skate till then and return here after he got off work, too. Maybe Peter would show up by then.

Gabe was skating again, and a few other kids had shown up, bringing the roomy skatepark alive with action. Kwasi raised his head from his desk now and again to observe the skaters through his glass window. He'd let Bruce change the radio station.

Whether it was Aaron's presence or the lack of Peter's usual encouragement, Jake was putting on a poor show. He kept losing his board in the middle of tricks, or having to jump off it to avoid falling. Frustration built as incompetence plagued him. Even stuff he could normally pull off without thinking was backfiring on him. After a while, he could barely stop himself from hurling his board across the room. His mother wouldn't have approved of the language tumbling from his mouth. This was a far cry from his performance the other day, when Marco had seen him.

By the time he'd kicked his board so furiously that it ran into Lex's cowboy boots across the cavernous park, Jake knew it was time to stop and rest. Everyone had bad runs, but how could he jog himself out of this rotten stretch? He walked over to retrieve his board from Lex and recoiled when the man tried to pat him comfortingly on the head.

He rushed to a bench on the other side of the floor, sat down, and peered back just long enough to see Lex standing there with a hurt look on his face. Jake shuddered.

He rested his head on his knees and closed his eyes for a moment. Man, he was wiped, and that didn't say much for his fitness level. Maybe he needed to take up jogging or something. Or maybe he was going to be useless all day for no good reason.

A soft bump on his bench indicated that someone had seated himself beside Jake. Not wanting to talk to anyone, Jake didn't look up.

"It's all in the mind, Jake," came Kwasi's soft voice. "You have to lean into it, ride with it, know what it's made of."

Jake raised his head but didn't turn it Kwasi's way. "Speak English, Kwasi."

"Mostly," Kwasi said, "you have to know what it's made of. Your resistance, that is."

Jake didn't like where this was going. He glared at the floor and considered getting up and walking away.

"You think I'm not trying?" he finally said, louder than he intended.

"No, I think you're trying too hard. You need a focus, one that eclipses the resistance, rather than wearing yourself out trying to beat up the resistance."

That did it. Jake jumped up, grabbed his board, and moved to another bench. He wasn't going to put up with psychobabble. You'd think a pro might actually have some practical tips to offer. But no, Kwasi was turning out to be as loony as his rehabs.

Annoyed or not, though, Jake was not a quitter. And he needed to redeem himself on a few moves. So when Kwasi disappeared back into his office, Jake took up his board and began ripping up and down the course. He scored a few small victories on tricks he'd blown before the sit-down, but things still weren't flowing.

As he paused and wiped a hand down his sweat-soaked T-shirt, a tap on the shoulder startled him. He turned.

"Jake, you need to turn your shoulders when you're going for a backtail," Aaron said, face stern as ever.

"Check it out." He dropped his board and demonstrated, exaggerating his shoulders on a backtail.

"And don't forget to set your feet," Bruce added with the flash of a smile.

Jake hesitated.

"Do it," Aaron commanded like someone accustomed to barking out orders.

Jake jumped on his board, focused on planting his feet, and cruised toward the ledge. Up shot his deck, his feet still aboard, then he managed a tailslide. Down he came, to his first smooth landing of the day.

"You've got it," Aaron said, face still serious.

"Thanks," Jake said, tongue-tied.

"Oh, and don't mind Kwasi," Bruce said. "He can't help playing doctor, you know. But his coaching advice is…"

"…*Right on!*" Aaron joined in with Bruce, mimicking Kwasi's favorite expression. The two threw back their heads and laughed. Jake began with a chuckle, then felt unrestrained laughter take hold. It felt good, really good, to share a belly laugh with these two.

"Just wait till you see him skate," came a third voice. Jake, Aaron, and Bruce turned to see Gabe joining their little huddle.

"When have you seen him skate?" Aaron asked. "He told me he doesn't skate much anymore."

Gabe drew a can of cola from his shorts pocket,

popped the tab, and took a long swig as if he hadn't heard Aaron's question. "Stole this from Lex," he declared. "He has a box of them. Uses them to clean the floors, on Kwasi's orders. Makes the ramps sticky, not slippery. You gotta be quick to get them behind Lex's back, though."

"I said, when does Kwasi skate?" Aaron demanded.

"Midnight. Only at midnight."

7   Peter's Day

Peter loved all-you-can-eat buffets, and this one was the bomb. He piled his plate high and offered a charming smile to the very young waitress passing by with a tray of desserts. Ha! He got a shy smile back.

"So, Peter," his dad was saying as they seated themselves, "you were saying you're going to show us the new half-pipe you built behind Sam's before you give us a tour of the skatepark? And you need to practice this afternoon for tomorrow's event?"

"That's right, Dad," Peter said, "but I'll be back to the hotel for dinner. Where'd you say we were going for dinner?"

"A five-star restaurant to celebrate your shot at a movie role," his mother teased.

"Better wait till Sunday night for celebrating."

"Of course, and I'll invite Sandra and Jake and Alyson to join us."

"Sandra might be available, but Jake and Alyson will be out with their grandmother."

"Oh? Sandra's mother is in town?"

"No, *Mr.* Evans's mother."

Richard and Laura Montpetit exchanged glances. "Has she heard anything?" Laura ventured.

"No," Peter said, stirring the ice in his drink slowly.

"Such a tragedy," his mother said.

"I still think he'll come home one day," Richard Montpetit declared.

Laura closed her hand over her husband's. Peter decided he didn't want dessert after all.

After a few minutes' silence, his mother said, "So, Peter, how's the studying for that entrance exam going?"

"No worries, Mom. I'll ace it. And I love that memory tricks book you picked up. Kwasi's going to teach me even more. They're good for skateboarding heats, you know."

"But you've been studying the practice exams, too?"

"Of course." Definitely no dessert. His waitress was gone, anyway. "Thanks a ton for brunch, Mom and Dad. First stop, Sam's."

They arrived there an hour before Jake was due to start work. As his parents chatted with Nancy, Peter wandered out back. First he noticed the black streaks down both sides of the half-pipe. Then he noticed a small hole in the ramp. He rushed over to pop his head underneath the tranny. Though no expert at inspections, he right away spotted two boards loose.

"BMXers," he muttered. Jake was going to freak. But it was still standing. Nothing too serious to repair — this round. He walked back into Sam's garage.

"Peter," Nancy said, "a word with you alone, please?"

Uh-oh. She *had* approved him not coming in for two days, hadn't she?

"Peter, I'm a little worried about Alyson's friends."

"Alyson's friends?"

"Yes. I'll mention it to Jake when he comes in, too. I don't mind her waiting here for Jake at the end of the day, of course. And I don't mind him giving her skateboard lessons in the back. But these BMX friends that Jake apparently arranged to give her the BMX lessons, well, they strike me as a little rough." Nancy reached a hand around to the nape of her neck to tug on her long, dark hair distractedly. "It's not my job to check up on her, you know, but I just thought I'd mention it. I like Alyson. She's a gutsy kid, isn't she? You should see the tricks she's doing on the half-pipe already."

"On the half-pipe? On a BMX bike?"

"Yes." Nancy was watching his face intently. Peter was speechless.

"Peter," his father called out, seeing that Nancy and Peter had finished their conversation. "Mind if we hurry out of here? I told an old friend I'd drop in on him at one o'clock, and we still need to see your half-pipe and get you to the skatepark for your workout."

Peter looked Nancy in the eye. "Definitely talk to Jake about this," he urged.

As it turned out, Peter managed to fit in two good hours of excellent skating that afternoon. Aaron, Bruce, and Gabe kept to themselves, as always, neither hassling nor helping him. *Détente*, Peter thought. That's what his social studies teacher would call it: when nations stop being enemies, but aren't yet friends.

When he allowed himself a break to cool down and let his ankles recoup, he saw Kwasi amble over.

"Peter, you're looking fine."

"Thanks, Kwasi. Any tips? My three-flip landings are a little sketch sometimes."

"Only once or twice. Try focusing on your board."

"Agreed. Kwasi, who's the dude hanging out with Lex over there?" Peter motioned to a boy about eighteen hovering near the cowboy cleaner.

"Oh, Billy. He's another TBI — sorry, traumatic brain injury rehab client. He's taking over from Lex after Saturday."

"Yeah? Where's our Lex off to? I was just getting used to him."

"Got a permanent job cleaning out stalls at a farm near here. An excellent placement for him. I'm really pleased."

"And what's with Billy?" Peter knew Kwasi loved to talk about his rehabs.

Kwasi shook his head sadly. "Billy was a sick BMXer who went OTB and smashed his head on a rock. No helmet."

Peter grimaced. OTB: over the handlebars of his bike. Gruesome.

"He's come a long way. For months, he could hardly speak, slept most of the day, and showed no emotion. He still tires easily and can't remember minute-to-minute what needs doing without a list written out. But I'm working with him."

"Kwasi, if these guys are not totally with it in their brains, how can you count on them to check screws and stuff?"

"Ah, you have to understand how memory works to know that. There's long-term memory — what happened before the accident — and short-term memory: what has happened since, or what you tried to learn today. TBIs often lose one of these, but not both, and sometimes they regain part of their memory over a period of months or years."

"So they can remember how to mop a floor or check screws if they did that kind of thing before they got hurt, but they have trouble learning new things?"

"Exactly. Or sometimes the other way around. I once heard of a medical doctor who could remember how to do surgery, but couldn't remember her own name. And she was devastated when they wouldn't let her do surgery."

"Well, I guess these people are lucky to have you helping them get back to a working life. Though a playing life is way more fun." With that, Peter grinned, leapt up, and went back to skating his heart out. He pulled out all the stops when he noticed that Aaron had left. Was he, Peter, ready to show up Aaron tomorrow? Peter was pretty sure it was within his reach.

Unfortunately, his mom and dad arrived before Jake did. Jake must have gotten held up at Sam's. Maybe he was mending the half-pipe. Never mind. They'd see each other tomorrow before the big event.

8   Tryouts

Jake wrestled long and hard with whether he should tell his mother what Alyson had been up to. He could hardly believe his sister had been sneaking around behind his back with a pack of guys even Jake and Peter knew better than to tangle with. He was stunned at how she'd told a bald-faced lie to Nancy, and furious that she'd given Judd and his crew permission to bike on his half-pipe. All because they'd offered to give her lessons when he hadn't shown up. Twice.

He could kick himself for that. It was the real reason he'd given in to her pleas not to report the matter to Mom. Instead, he'd made her promise not to let Judd and his buddies on the half-pipe ever again, and had embarrassed both himself and Alyson by confessing the situation to Nancy so that she'd be on the lookout for both the BMXers and any unscheduled hanging out on Alyson's part. He'd also forced Alyson to help him repair the half-pipe and put up a "no trespassing" sign. Like that was going to stop them now, he groused.

Despite the new tension between them, he'd agreed to give Alyson a quick lesson at the skatepark this morning before it shut down for afternoon try-outs. Nancy, knowing that Jake wanted to get in some final practice before the event, had given him the entire day off.

"Marco had some say in that, too," she'd revealed.

Ever since Xtreme Sk8 had officially opened on Tuesday, it had been jammed with wannabe stunt-boys. Most were half Jake's and Peter's age, and as far as Jake was concerned, they were merely cluttering up the place.

Luckily, Kwasi allowed Jake, Peter, Alyson, Aaron, Bruce, and Gabe the run of the park before and after closing time if they knocked, in exchange for their continued help on projects. The number of jobs needing doing had grown steadily that week as Kwasi prepared to host Marco's event.

So when Jake and Alyson rapped on the door at seven sharp, Kwasi let them in without hesitation.

"Ah, the first members of my secret Xtreme Team," he enthused. "I'm surprised all six of you aren't here already. Alyson, are you trying out for stuntgirl?"

She giggled. "Yeah, right."

"Well, don't let me hold you up. We shut down at

eleven, remember, and I sure could use your help from then till the tryouts at one. By the way, the actors who are playing the skateboarders in Marco's movie will be here this afternoon. Jake, you must meet one of them: Karl. You'll see why."

Jake shrugged, puzzled but not willing to show interest. "We'll help from eleven to one, Kwasi. Alyson too."

"Right on!" How did Jake know he was about to say that?

Aaron and crew filed in at 7:45, half an hour after the rehabs, Lex and Billy. Jake avoided all of them, taking turns working with Alyson, and practicing a string of tricks when she asked to rest. At one point, when he thought she'd taken off for the restroom, he was surprised to see her arguing vigorously with Kwasi in the office. Kwasi looked half amused, half ticked off. Jake was about to stride over there when Alyson turned and stomped back toward Jake.

This brink-of-teenhood thing was getting out of hand. Was she trying to negotiate BMX time at Sk8? Hadn't she already figured out that ramps built for skateboarders rarely hold up long to the punishment of BMXers' pedals and pegs? The pegs were small metal bars that poked out from the wheels so riders could grind down rails and stall on ledges. He sighed. Kwasi was probably way more qualified to handle Alyson's sudden new personality than he was.

Peter showed up at ten o'clock, unconcerned that he had only an hour's skating left. "I'm conserving my energy for this afternoon," he said to Jake. "Have you seen Marco's postings on who goes in what order?"

"Nope."

"I'm one of the first. You're in the middle. Aaron is one of the last."

"Is that a good thing?"

"Doesn't matter," his buddy said confidently. Jake wished he had a fraction of Peter's confidence, feigned or real. But the morning had gone well, he admitted, and it wasn't like he had to get a movie part anyway. He just didn't want to make a fool of himself in public. He wanted to be the best he could be. Oh, man, that sounded way too much like a Kwasi line.

"When are Bruce and Gabe competing?" he asked.

"Kwasi's letting Bruce do the music. I didn't notice Gabe on the list."

"Oh," Jake said. Interesting that Bruce wasn't competing, but that boy sure did like Kwasi's music system. The noise in the skatepark was almost unbearable by one o'clock. Jake, Alyson, and the boys had been hauling and setting up with Lex and Billy for two hours. Gabe's cheek bruise was looking better and, for once, he was wearing a shirt, Jake noticed. Now crowds were fast filling the stands, and Marco, looking suave in a silver vest over a dress shirt and tailored trousers, was watching someone do final checks on the sound system. Then he took the mike in hand and spoke.

"Good afternoon, and an especially warm welcome to all the keen skateboarders here today. How about a cheer before we start for Kwasi Kumar, the manager of Chilliwack's brand-new Xtreme Sk8park, for hosting and helping to organize this event."

Jake scanned the spectators, located Alyson clapping enthusiastically in the middle of the crowd. She caught his eye and waved. That lifted a tiny corner of the dark cloud he'd been moving in since he'd awakened.

Don't think about it. Don't think about this day three years ago.

"So, ladies and gentlemen," Marco continued, "each skateboarder will participate in two heats, or runs of tricks. Tomorrow, I'll announce the two winners and an alternate. The alternate will perform in the movie only if one of the two stuntboys falls ill or gets injured."

Jake spotted Peter's parents, overdressed for a skatepark, holding hands. He wondered if his mother would make it in time to see him.

"…and let the show begin!"

As music blared from the speakers, Jake shot a glance at the office to see Bruce grinning as if he'd won the lottery.

Jake craned his neck to watch the first pint-sized

skateboarder whiz across the room and begin laying on tricks. The crowd "oohed" when he tried a huge kickflip, and made sympathetic noises when he tumbled off his board.

Jake could see that Peter, standing third in line, had his eyes locked on Marco's face. He was judging his reaction to each of the skaters and waiting for his signal. When it came, he sped onto the stage, back foot pumping till he lifted it gracefully onto his board and zoomed up the first ramp. Then he did a nollie k-grind down the hubba, ollieing off his board's nose, then performing a crooked grind, his front truck at a slight angle.

He was a born performer, Jake had to admit. Not only could he pull off a staggering repertoire of tricks, but he delivered each with the flair of an Olympic athlete. Every twist, turn, and moment of flight, he and his board were one. Jake stole a glance at Marco. Intensely taking it in — and suitably impressed. But there was still Aaron to consider. And — Jake let his breath out slowly to blow away another corner of that hovering cloud — there was himself. Yes, if he was right on the money and Aaron wasn't, he had a chance. But did he, Jake, really want it?

Jake turned to see Gabe beside him, no board in hand.

"When's your heat?" Jake asked.

"Not competing."

"Not going for it?"

Gabe shrugged. "Not too late for you to pull out," he said.

Jake looked at him but couldn't read his expression.

"Your parents up there?" Gabe asked after a moment, jerking his head toward the stands.

Jake hesitated. "My mom might make it."

Gabe studied Jake. "Yeah, that's right. I heard Peter tell Kwasi that your old man ran out on you."

Jake felt his cheeks go hot. His fingernails pressed into his palms.

But he wouldn't give Gabe the satisfaction of a reply. He would not. Gabe's eyes continued to scan his face.

"No big. Dads are definitely overrated," Gabe said. Then he was gone, absorbed by the milling crowd.

What was that supposed to mean? Jake stewed, then slowly smiled. Of course. Gabe saw Jake as a possible threat to his buddy Aaron. So he was trying to rattle him or persuade him not to compete. That made his meddling a compliment. Didn't it?

All too soon, it was Jake's turn. He put his board in motion, trying to flash through his mind all the tricks he'd worked out. Maybe he should have had a look at Peter's memory tricks book. Up the spine he went, and down the other side. A hop up to the railing. A feeble grind. Yikes. His board clipped just before he was ready to land, and he bailed.

He retrieved his board, stepped up, and pulled off a hardflip (an inward heelflip). He was doing it, but not with the flair and confidence he intended. Next was the backside lipslide (ollieing up and over a boardslide), then the bluntslide, then what? His throat tightened so much he could hardly breathe as he zoomed up the vert ramp, flailed mid-air, and dropped. The board snuck out from under him for a second time, sending him sliding. Shaken now, Jake retrieved it, skipped the next two tricks he had planned, and pulled off a trio of tech manuals. The crowd clapped politely, but Jake wanted to keep skating right out of the park, head down. He slunk to the back of the lineup. Was Marco counting both heats, or the best one? Could Jake pull it together for the second round? He felt a tug on his arm.

"Jake, stop looking like you did something terrible. You made two small mistakes, and your backlip was awesome," Alyson said. "The crowd loved it, but I bet you couldn't even hear them, you were so busy being down on yourself."

Jake sighed. "Al, I can't do this today."

She squinted up at him. "Jake, what would Kwasi say if he were back here right now coaching you?"

Jake snorted. "Kwasi? He'd say 'Eclipse your resistance, Jake, instead of beating against it.'" Jake looked at Alyson, expecting her to giggle. Instead, she scratched her head, stared at the stands for a moment, then unexpectedly flung her arms around her brother. Although her head came only to his chest, he heard her next words as if they were in his ear.

"Do it for Dad, Jake. Do it to make him proud." She released him and sprinted back to the stands.

Jake stared at her retreating back. He lost sight of her for a second — it didn't help that his eyes were stinging. When he relocated her, he glimpsed her hugging his mom, who'd just arrived.

"Jake Evans," Marco was saying over the system.

Jake squeezed his eyes shut, opened them, and moved forward reciting his list of moves: Feeble (riding on his back wheels with his front truck wheels hooked over), smith (using just the back wheels, the front wheels hanging below), hardflip, backlip, blunt, and manuals. One by one he moved through them, concentrating on effecting smooth transitions between them, projecting confidence for the blurred crowd. Hardflip, blunt, manuals. One to go. He leaned into his backlip. *Lean into it, ride with it, know what it's made of.*

He pushed faster than he'd ever pushed. He could feel a smooth landing waiting for him, guaranteed somehow.

The thump the board made on landing was

drowned out by the crowd. This time he heard the spectactors' full roar. As he headed back to the wings, he raised a hand the way medallists do at the Olympics. It wasn't for show, although it whipped the crowd's cheers to a higher volume. It was a wave to someone that he wished, how he wished, was in the stands watching somehow.

As Jake paused in the shadows at one end of the building, Peter, Alyson, and his mother all crashed into him at the same time.

"You were awesome, awesome, awesome, old buddy," Peter was shouting, punching him in the shoulder. "Where the heck have you been hiding all those moves?"

Jake just smiled. Smiled and clutched Al and his mother for a fraction longer than he meant to.

"I'm proud of you," his mother said.

"You did it," Alyson added, jumping high enough to plant a kiss on his cheek.

"Aaron's on," Peter broke in. That sent Alyson scurrying back to the stands, and Sandra waving as she retreated to the entrance to return to work.

Together, Jake and Peter watched Aaron rocket onto the floor in his trademark black, including his shiny helmet. He attacked the obstacles like a gladiator, moving from one end to another, killing everything in his wake. He was pouring himself into every trick.

But as he moved to his specialty, the bowls, a commotion at the front doors drew the boys' heads away.

Not one, but four BMX bikes flowed through the double doors and spread out among the ramps. Aaron, frozen on the bowl's deck with his board dangling limply from his hand, looked from the approaching bikers to Marco, whose mouth was hanging open. The BMXers raced from one end of the building to the other, leaping and bucking like wild ponies, performing tricks everywhere they went.

Half the crowd was cheering. The other half was jeering. From the corner of his eye, Jake saw Kwasi sprint from the office to the nearest BMXer and grab his handlebars as he sped past. The rider shoved Kwasi away hard and escaped to perform another trick, to wild clapping and cheering from a section of young boys near the front. Just as fast, Kwasi sprinted toward another biker, which sent streams of kids onto the floor, chasing the poachers. Jake saw Lex and Billy dash into the confusion from the other side of the floor.

"Everyone stop. Would everyone please freeze and stay calm until Xtreme Sk8 staff escort the BMXers out," Marco's voice was attempting to say over the public announcement system. But no one paid any attention.

The BMXers clearly had friends in the crowd because some had emerged to act as bodyguards. They were preventing kids from reaching the uninvited competitors. One even grabbed Marco's mike from him and began narrating the BMXers' tricks like a master of ceremonies until someone tackled him to the floor of Marco's podium.

Soon the entire floor had turned into a confused meleé, with some spectators in danger of being crushed by stampedes both onto the floor and out the door.

Alyson, Jake thought. He tried to make his way toward the stands. But there was no moving anywhere in this bedlam. He looked to where Alyson had been, only to see Billy lift her from a fall and help her out the door. Jake began using his elbows to move toward the entrance.

One by one, the BMXers were being brought down by groups of excited youths, but one remained on the bowls, guarded by a ring of accomplice protectors and a contingent of boys wildly encouraging his wheelies and grinds. Jake watched as Judd's bike charged up the tranny and hovered high in the air, as poised as an eagle ready to make a kill. But something else was also flying through the air.

A lasso! The coil of rope encircled Judd, yanked tight into a noose around his chest, and hauled him down before gravity had a chance to play out the last half of his aerial performance. Thump! Jake winced. The startled biker landed heavily on his side, feet still on his bike pedals. Like every other head in the park,

Jake's swiveled to take in Lex holding the other end of the rope, arm raised in victory to thunderous applause. A dozen boys crashed through the wall of bouncers to separate Judd from his bike.

Jake saw Kwasi fighting to regain control of the mike when police sirens sounded, drowning out all other noise as police rushed into the complex. One officer raised a megaphone and began shouting orders. Others fought their way to the huddles of kids laying into the downed BMXers.

Jake kept trying to maneuver to the door through which Billy had carried his sister. He finally found her around the side of the building, sobbing as Billy hovered over her.

"Alyson, are you hurt?" He saw a bruise on one shin, took in her wide, frightened eyes, and watched her determined efforts to pull herself together. She shook her head no as Billy stared at Jake, unblinking. Jake checked her over to make sure. As Billy continued to stare at him, Jake forced himself to straighten his back and look Billy in the eye. He cleared his throat, took a step closer to the boy.

"Hi, Billy. I'm Jake, Alyson's brother."

"I know," Billy replied promptly.

"Thanks for helping her out here. You must be pretty strong to have done that." He couldn't quite bring himself to offer Billy his hand, but Billy didn't seem to expect it.

"Hey, I'm not that heavy," Alyson protested.

Billy broke into a wide smile and said, "No problem, bud. Smokin' run on your last heat." He turned and headed back into the skatepark, a slight limp in his gait.

"Did you know anything about the BMXers coming?" Jake couldn't stop himself from asking Alyson.

"No." She shook her head vigorously and wiped an arm across her wet eyes.

It wasn't like Alyson to cry, especially in public. He gave her another quick hug, then looked up as an ambulance arrived, and several police officers helped injured spectators and bikers out of the building and into the ambulance.

"Guess Judd and his friends are thinking they had their fun," Jake said aloud. He also thought, *Poor Kwasi. Poor Marco.*

Alyson hung her head.

"Folks. Come on back in. The show will go on," Kwasi's voice boomed from the front doors. "Let's show the party crashers that they didn't close us down."

Jake looked at Alyson. She nodded and they helped herd people milling about the front entrance back inside.

Kwasi appeared. "Jake, Alyson. You okay? Great. Marco is on the mike inside, trying to get things rolling again. Lex, Billy, Bruce, and Gabe have been checking the ramps for damage. A few surface tears at one end, not enough to shut things down, and Billy has been tightening up some screws that worked their way loose. We're good to go again."

"We're coming," Alyson said. "Have to see who wins, don't we?"

Jake checked out the stands. Not nearly as many people as earlier, but folks were still streaming back in. Marco's voice was steady and sure.

"Ladies and gentlemen, let us not allow an unfortunate disruption to spoil the day for the competitors, who have voted to carry on this afternoon. Put your hands together, skateboard fans, for Aaron Glicksberg."

Jake, with Alyson right behind him, located Peter and headed over to him. The three seated themselves and glued their eyes on the figure in black poised exactly where he had been the minute before the BMX storm had unleashed itself. Peter's back was as straight as the wall behind them, Jake observed. His hands gripped the bleacher seat beneath him. All business, Jake thought. As if nothing had just gone down. Jake himself was having a hard time concentrating. His mind refused to refocus from the past twenty minutes' craziness to the tryouts. As Aaron began moving through his tricks, Jake gradually sensed that he was having the same problem. Oh, he was still smooth by most standards. He was still going for almost every move invented. But microscopic hesitations and stumbles revealed that Aaron the Ace was a little rattled, not in usual form.

Jake's heartbeat quickened as he watched Aaron go for a kickflip back tailslide, catch an edge, and slide out. Smoothly, as if it was part of the choreography, the boy leapt up, climbed back on his board, and whipped up the nearest deck. But as he dropped in, he lost it and "ate poop," as skateboarders say.

Peter shifted. Jake locked his hands together in his lap. Though Jake would never dare admit it to Peter, he felt totally sorry for Aaron. Whose head wouldn't be a little messed up after what had just gone down?

"Thirty seconds left," Marco's voice pronounced.

As Aaron lay sprawled on the flat bottom, Kwasi sprinted toward him, first-aid belt strapped around his waist. The audience strained their necks. Aaron moved just before Kwasi reached him, raised his hand to signal he was okay, and rose with the help of Kwasi's strong arms. As he managed to walk slowly off the floor on his own steam, the crowd cheered. But Jake shook his head. The situation sucked. It was rotten luck. And yet, even if it hadn't been classic Aaron, the skating had been powerful. If Marco padded his judging with a little sympathy, Aaron's performance was still possibly impressive enough to edge out the rest. One glance at Peter's face told Jake that Peter wasn't so sure who had won, either.

As Marco repeated his announcement that the winners' names would be posted early the next morning, people began filing out. Jake longed to go home and collapse. He was physically and emotionally exhausted, even without the prospect of having dinner with his grandmother tonight. But Kwasi had extracted a promise from his so-called Xtreme Team to help clear up, so Jake, Peter, and Alyson began going through the motions. As always, the other half of the "team" avoided and ignored them. The tension was thicker than ever, yet Kwasi pretended not to notice as he glided between the two sets, chatting and directing their work.

Finally Kwasi said, "That's it, boys and Alyson. Thanks a ton for all your work. Don't forget to say goodbye to Lex. It's his last day."

This prompted Bruce to stride over to Kwasi's office. Kwasi raised an eyebrow, but said nothing as the sound system clicked on and Bruce slipped in a CD, then turned the volume sky high.

Lex jerked his head up and giggled. Billy slapped Lex on the back. Kwasi's body began to sway like he couldn't stop it, and even Aaron and his gang were having a hard time stifling smiles.

Jake wasn't much on country music, but even he

had heard the Garth Brooks and Chris Ledoux lyrics before. So, like everyone else, he joined in as Bruce poked his head out the office door and began belting out the words:

> *Watcha' gonna do with a cowboy when that old*
> *rooster crows at dawn…*
> *Don't even start to think you're gonna change him*
> *You'd be better off to try and rope the wind,*
> *What you see is what he's got*
> *And he can't be what he's not*

For the first and only moment that day, Jake relaxed and was part of something beyond the day's rivalries, tensions, and suffocating memories.

"Watcha' gonna do with a cowboy?" he finished the tune with the rest of the Xtreme Team singers.

9   We're It!

As it turned out, Peter's parents had to leave very early Sunday morning to catch planes in Seattle, so Peter had them drop him off at Xtreme Sk8 instead of at Jake's. He should really have waited for Jake to be up and ready to cruise over with him to see if the notice was up, but the suspense had been killing him all night. He couldn't wait another minute. He'd just tell Jake he hadn't wanted to wake up the Evans household at that hour.

Unfortunately, the notice wasn't on the door yet. Peter kicked a loose stone away from the front door in frustration. It landed in the shallow concrete bowl of the outdoor park, in the center of a giant "A." Peter looked closer. The "A" was part of graffiti spelling out "Aaron." The words "Bruce" and "Gabe," if you could decipher graffiti scrawl, colored the rest of the bowl in bright spray-painted colors outlined by gold. Some nerve these guys had, applying graffiti to a brand-new bowl. What was Kwasi going to do about that? Then again, Kwasi was just strange enough that he might have let them. Like a naturalist bent on observing wolves marking their territory, Peter thought wryly.

He moved closer to the door, put his ear to it. Silly, really, since Kwasi never showed before seven. But what was that? The rumble of a skateboard. Someone was in there skating. At six a.m.?

He knocked. The rumble stopped, but no one came to the door. Maybe he'd just imagined it. Might have been the air conditioning kicking in. He knocked louder, pounded. Nothing. Curious, Peter decided to walk around the building. There were no windows, no bushes, just dirt and new grass trying to grow in. As he rounded the rear of the building, he noticed a giant vent slightly askew. The screws had come off one corner. Had a little kid tried to break in through a vent, or had the construction crew not screwed it down very tightly? Not a big deal, since it's unlikely anyone would make it through that opening, but he made a mental note to mention it to Kwasi. As he rounded the corner that put him back at the front, he was surprised to see a tall, middle-aged man with a hard face, wearing workboots, jeans, and work shirt, rapping on the front door. The man cradled a hard hat in one arm. Hadn't the construction guys finished up already?

Peter coughed. The man swung around and dropped the hand that had been knocking on the door.

"Doesn't open till nine, but the manager is usually here at seven," Peter informed the laborer, who suddenly looked ill at ease.

"Nine, eh?" he said, donning the hat, stuffing his hands into his pockets, and eyeing Peter suspiciously. "Okay, then. Nice place, isn't it? Great place for kids to hang out."

Peter opened his mouth to reply, but the man spun around and walked off, hands fishing for a cigarette, lighting it as he strolled away with what struck Peter as a studied nonchalance.

Peter stroked his chin thoughtfully. Must be the dad of a kid who'd competed yesterday, looking for the posting. Someone who thought his kid was going to be in the movies. *Sorry*, Peter thought, *but it's all wrapped up. I hope.* He planted his ear against the door one more time, heard nothing, and turned toward Jake's house, mouth watering for a full Evans breakfast.

An hour later, sausages and eggs nestled comfortably in his gut, Peter biked alongside Jake to the skatepark.

"How was your dinner last night?" he ventured.

"Got through it," Jake replied in a flat tone that put a lid on any other questions Peter might have had.

"Supposed to be bright and sunny today. Hope we

get to guide on the river this afternoon, not work in the smelly garage," he ventured.

"Sam has all the rafts booked today; we'll definitely be on the river," Jake confirmed. "But if Kwasi's in, we can skate till we're due over there."

Peter barely heard the last comment because he'd spotted the piece of paper taped to the door and was sprinting like a World Cup biker within sight of a finish line. He dropped his bike and lunged at the door.

"Yahoo!" he screeched. "Jake, Jake, can you believe it? Jake, get your butt over here!"

Jake seemed to take forever to reach his side. Peter watched his buddy's face scan the paper, his jaw loosen, his eyes meet Peter's. He looked more amazed than happy. Peter grabbed Jake and shook him.

"We're it, old buddy! We're it! Can you believe it? It's perfect! We made it! We're a team! You and me!"

"And Aaron as alternate."

"Yup!"

"He's not going to be pleased."

"So what? Fair's fair. Marco is the man. Jake, will you smile or something? You're a stuntboy. You're going to be in a movie. You're going to get paid to skate in front of cameras." He watched a smile spread across Jake's face. *Finally.* The poor guy seemed to be in shock. To be honest, Peter was a little surprised too, but Jake had skated really solidly his second heat yesterday. He'd laid down some sick trick combos. He'd earned this, and it saved Peter from having to work with someone he didn't know or like.

"I am *so* stoked, Jake. We are so going to have fun. What are we going to do to celebrate this?"

"Hey, way to go, guys," a voice said from behind. Peter turned to see Bruce, on his own for once. He was holding his skateboard and fingering the chains dangling from his neck. His smile was real. "Must've been those tunes I laid on for you, eh?"

Peter glanced beyond Bruce to see if Aaron was in sight. "You were the best DJ in the house, Bruce. Looked like you were having fun."

"Door's unlocked," Bruce said, pushing it open.

The three entered and looked toward the office. Kwasi and Gabe were in there, so wrapped up in conversation they didn't even wave. Bruce, Jake, and Peter dropped their boards and began skating.

"Quite the scene yesterday, eh?" Bruce said, legs pumping his board with full energy as he skated alongside Peter. "Wonder if any of the BMXers got injured?"

"Jake's mom works at the hospital. She said that Judd, the guy Lex lassoed, was brought to the emergency room, but released pretty fast. No broken ribs, just bruises," Peter responded, pleased that Bruce was being friendly. He'd always suspected Bruce was the okay one, if separated from his buddies.

"That'll teach him to show up at parties he's not invited to."

"Uh-huh. Aaron coming in today?"

"Don't think so."

Peter waited, but Bruce didn't elaborate.

"Hey," Bruce said, "we were planning on doing some street skating tomorrow at midnight. You and Jake into street stuff?"

"Street stuff? Like where?"

"We know some places with no security guards."

"Sounds interesting," Peter said cautiously. "Let me ask Jake later."

"We'll be taking off from here at eleven thirty."

"Gotcha." Peter glanced over at Jake, who was working the bowls. So, did "we" mean Bruce and Gabe, or all three of those guys? And was this a crack in the ice, or a set-up? He wasn't at all sure Jake would be into it. He did know that Mrs. Evans wasn't working night shift tomorrow night. But the boys could always sneak out the bedroom window. And skating uptown might be fun. If anyone objected, they'd just scatter.

"Kwasi, where's the music, man?" Bruce shouted across the room. Kwasi, still locked in some kind of heavy conference with Gabe, looked up but barely nodded and didn't turn the system on right away. But eventually, the tunes spilled into the room, about the same time that Gabe emerged.

Peter did a double take. Gabe must have had a heck of a fall. One eye was nearly swollen shut and black as coal. It wasn't from all the pushing and shoving at yesterday's tryouts. Peter knew this because Gabe had been busy checking for damage underneath the constructions during the craziness, and the only bruise on his face when he'd left was from that slam a couple of days ago — the one he'd mentioned to Jake.

Peter turned away quickly as Gabe shot him a hostile look for staring, only to find Bruce at his elbow, also studiously looking the other way.

"He took a bad one, hey?" Peter said too quietly for his voice to carry to Gabe.

"No guts, no glory, I guess," Bruce replied. "He's one dedicated dude. He's always the first here, and the last to leave. Sometimes I think he wouldn't even go home if Kwasi didn't lock up."

Peter nodded, but wondered. For the number of hours Gabe skated, he wasn't all that hot, and he didn't seem to love it, like the rest of the boys. He was just there, going through the motions, and interacting as little as possible with anyone else.

A few minutes later, Kwasi hustled over to Peter. "Peter, I'm stoked for you. You and Jake are it. Right on!" He slapped Peter's shoulder and grinned like a guy in a toothpaste commercial. Peter couldn't help smiling back. There was nothing fake about Kwasi's high-energy smiles.

"Thanks, Kwasi. Must be that great coaching I had. You going to coach any of the movie shoots themselves? Marco's notice says the first shoot is here, tomorrow afternoon."

"Not that I know of, but hey," he rubbed his fingers together and smiled teasingly, "if Marco opens his wallet, I coach. Got to keep my wreck of a car running somehow."

Peter smiled. "Kwasi, I've been wondering, how come you never skate with us? I've never seen you skate, you know."

Kwasi eyed Peter's skateboard like he was tempted to step on it right there, but he grinned even wider, winked, and said, "I'm on duty, young man. But fear not. You'll see me skate sometime."

Then he glanced at his watch and cracked a frown. "Billy's late."

"Is that a big deal?" Peter asked, distracted by Jake hurling up four feet over the bowl and smacking his tail on the way down.

"Well, it means he's struggling with his system for remembering where he has to be when, and that will make it hard for me to get him a quality work placement."

"Where do these guys live, anyway?" Peter asked, mildly curious. "Who looks after them?"

"Some have families. They're the ones who do best, though it's often difficult for the families to adjust to their needs. Some, like Billy, live in group homes where a trained support worker keeps an eye on them while encouraging them to be as independent as they can be. But that's expensive, and the ones with no family or financial support have the roughest time reintegrating into society."

"Kwasi, you use big words, but my guess is you'll be an awesome shrink," Peter declared. "You're one of those guys out to save the world."

Kwasi smiled. "And what are you out to do, Peter?"

Peter picked up his board, scanned the skatepark. "Get in the movies, Kwasi." He saw Kwasi's smile dim a shade.

"You remind me of Marco sometimes, Peter: single-minded and ambitious."

Peter felt his face flush with pride.

"But single-mindedness can lead to tunnel vision. The movie industry can be brutally shallow, my boy, and that's something I think you're not." He clapped a hand on Peter's shoulder, then nodded toward the door. "Here comes Billy. Better late than never."

Peter, amused as ever at the way Kwasi was always playing doctor, was happy to escape to the ramps. He was even happier when Bruce complimented him on some of his tricks. Soon he, Bruce, and Jake — Gabe listening and skating alongside — were so involved in chatting about favorite skateboard pros and movies that it was more than an hour before he stopped to check his watch. It was getting close to Sam time. Not that he really needed to work for Sam anymore, now that he was going to get $150 a day as a stuntboy. So sweet. But money wasn't even the important part. The important part, he thought as he watched Billy pull a notebook from his pocket, check off a chore, and fetch the broom, was impressing Marco, 'cause Marco was probably capable of taking him places. Like auditions for acting, maybe an agent. Yes, Peter had plans. Big plans. And whatever Kwasi said, they all revolved around impressing Marco.

10   Under the Bowls

When Jake and Peter showed up at Sk8 straight after their Sam's Adventure Tours shift, Alyson wasn't at the front door waiting for them as usual. Instead, Jake found her spraying window cleaner fluid on the office window, rubbing a cloth, giggling, and making faces through the window at Billy, who was doing the same from the other side of the glass.

Peter made for the opposite end of the park with his board.

"What a team!" Kwasi joked as Jake strolled over. "I'm not getting a thing done, but they sure are getting along."

His eyes surveyed Jake's face closely, prompting Jake to put on a big smile and say, "Hi, Billy. Working hard, I see. So, Al, ready to work on ollieing steps today?"

She took longer to extract herself from the office than he liked but was totally into the lesson once they were across the room. In fact, he could hardly believe how fast his sister was picking up tricks.

"You're killing it, Alyson," he said as she executed a power slide, the skater's equivalent of the skier's snowplow, or stopping by turning ninety degrees with a braking force.

"You're killing it," Billy echoed behind them, beaming at Alyson, who turned and gave him a warm look.

"Billy, don't you have some work to do?" Jake asked.

Billy fumbled for a notebook in his back pocket and read it with all the concentration of a student who had lost his place during a class reading.

"Screws," he said happily and ducked under a street-section wedge after pulling a screwdriver from the tool belt around his waist.

"Jake, have you ever been underneath the obstacles?" Alyson asked.

"Nope," he responded.

"Come see," Alyson said, grabbing his hand and tugging him toward the bowls. He smiled and decided to humor her. It was dark under the bowls, where a curved wall of two-by-fours dropped almost to the floor, creating a labyrinth of nooks and crannies. Alyson grabbed a flashlight hanging from a hook beside them, dropped to her hands and knees, and began crawling.

"Just like my half-pipe, but a bit bigger," Jake

observed. "And quality construction. Get a load of how well the joints fit."

"Great place for playing hide-and-seek. Remember how we used to play hide-and-seek?" Alyson replied, squirming like a caver ahead. "Hey, someone else has been playing hide-and-seek under here."

She'd stopped. Jake pushed forward on his stomach to follow her beam of light. There, where the half-pipe began to rise on the other side, was a little nest: blankets, a pillow, and a water bottle.

Jake pulled himself up to sit cross-legged beside the hideaway and looked at Alyson. "Think Billy hangs out here when Kwasi isn't looking?"

"Dunno," she said, grabbing a bag of sunflower seeds she'd spotted beside the blanket. She paused, then returned it to its place. "Maybe it was Lex's. Or maybe it's Kwasi's."

They both laughed at that, then turned around and crawled back to where the flashlight had been hanging.

"Hey! There you are!" Peter remarked, his head hanging from the deck above. "Bruce and Gabe are going to the subway sandwich place to eat. They invited us along. Gabe's gone home to get some money, and Bruce is waiting for us outside."

"Can we?" Alyson asked Jake. "Mom's out, and it would save you making supper."

Jake pulled his wallet from his back pocket and

scanned its contents quickly. He decided they'd be okay if he and Alyson shared a sandwich. Hopefully Peter would think they weren't very hungry. Then again, he remembered, he was going to get stuntboy pay next week.

"Sure," he said cheerfully.

"Can we invite Billy?"

Jake stared at her. "I don't think that's on his list, Alyson."

She didn't argue.

"Alright!" Bruce said as the four of them waved goodbye to Kwasi and Billy and took off. "Gabe's place is on the way. We'll stop and pick him up there."

A few minutes later, Jake, Peter, and Alyson hung back as Bruce rapped at the door of a bungalow that looked a lot like the Evans's. A big man in workboots, jeans, and work shirt answered the door. He glared at them.

"What do you want?"

"Is Gabe here, or did he leave already?" Bruce asked.

"He's here and going nowhere," the man snarled, making the boys and Alyson take steps backward. "Now move on outta here."

Four pairs of feet followed his advice quickly. As they settled themselves in a booth at the sandwich shop, Peter said, "I saw Gabe's dad earlier today, at Sk8. Guess he was looking for Gabe."

"His old man's mean," Bruce pronounced. "Hope Gabe can get away tomorrow for…"

"…for meeting us after the movie shoot?" Jake queried loudly, pointing to Alyson behind her back for Bruce's benefit. Bruce had almost given away their midnight plans.

"Yeah," Bruce said, picking up pickles that had fallen out of his sandwich and poking them back in. "You were looking good today, Alyson, inside and outside."

"You skated outside before I got there?" Jake asked. On whose board? he wondered.

He saw a look pass between Bruce and Alyson.

"Yes," Alyson said, voice defiant.

"She's dedicated," Bruce observed. "Too bad Marco doesn't need a stuntgirl."

Alyson giggled and Jake relaxed. *Guess I need to cut my sister some more slack,* he thought. She wasn't a little girl anymore, and secretly he was pretty proud of how fast she could pick up a new sport.

"I'm beat," Jake declared as he pushed away the empty wrapper from his sub. "Two skating sessions and a full day of work at Sam's in between."

"Me, too," Peter said. "Good thing Nancy has given us the rest of the week off. Not that she had much choice, since the movie shoot starts tomorrow."

"Wish they let people inside to watch," Bruce complained.

"Me, too, but right now, I think we'd better get home," Alyson said. "It's starting to rain."

"Rain?" Jake looked out the window, saw it was poised to become a downpour. "Uh-oh. I left my jacket at Sk8. You guys dash. I'll catch you at home."

"See you tomorrow," Bruce said, one eyebrow raised as if to signal "at midnight."

Peter and Alyson headed their bikes to Jake's house as Jake pedaled for Sk8. He got there just as Kwasi was locking up.

"Sorry, Kwasi, left my jacket," he apologized.

"And you'll certainly be needing that," Kwasi said, holding the door open for him.

Jake grabbed the jacket and paused. "Kwasi, Alyson and I were crawling under the big bowl this morning, just to see how it was made, and we found some blankets and a pillow. Maybe Lex had a hiding spot?"

Kwasi didn't reply right away. He seemed to be considering how to answer. "It's okay, Jake; I know. It's all under control."

This wasn't what Jake had expected. Kwasi's words and tone suddenly dropped a puzzle piece into place, revealing a full picture.

"Kwasi, is it Gabe's stuff?"

Kwasi turned penetrating eyes on Jake. For a second, Jake felt like he was in a doctor's office, getting a light shone in his eyes during a check-up.

"I said I know about the blankets, Jake."

"His dad beats him, right? That's why he's always bruised, not from skating? And you let him hide here when it gets bad?" Jake was putting it together as he said it. *Kwasi only skates at midnight.* How else would Gabe have known that? Words were tumbling out. "He told me dads are overrated. And Peter saw his dad looking for him at the park at six o'clock this morning. His dad wouldn't let him go out with us this evening. And Peter told me to tell you that someone has unscrewed the corner of the ventilation system in the back of the building."

Kwasi sighed. "Jake, I'm not sure what your future calling is, detective or shrink, but I appreciate your information and concern."

Jake waited. Kwasi sighed a second time, looking as bagged as Jake had ever seen him.

"Sometimes dads are overrated, and sometimes they just need help."

Psychobabble again. But Jake didn't run away this time, not even when he felt Kwasi rest a hand on his shoulder.

"You're a good kid, Jake. And that tells me a lot about your dad, whether he comes home or not."

11   The Perfect Double

Jake had never seen so many boxy white vans in his life. They seemed to have laid siege to Xtreme Sk8, along with endless coils of black, heavy-gauge electrical cable being unwound by workers shouting orders to one another. Some of the trailers had the words "dressing room" on the side. Fold-up steps led from their doors, which were opening and closing as people hustled around the site. Other trailers were wide open, revealing mountains of equipment ranging from ladders to pipe clamps and platform components. Beside two trailers marked "Craft Services," aproned workers were busy piling food onto tables. Everything from soda pop to salads, sandwich wraps and desserts to gum. Jake's mouth watered just looking at the feast.

He couldn't stop staring. All this for this after-noon's shoot inside the skatepark? Marco had ordered three half-days of skateboard shoots altogether, assuming all went well. Jake shook his head in disbelief. All this for a movie in which skateboarding was just one of the sports featured?

"Get used to it, old buddy. That food is for us. We're part of the cast. I think I need to pinch myself," Peter said, fingering the identification badge that hung around his neck. Marco's assistant had dropped off their badges the evening before.

They made their way to the front door of Sk8 and flashed their badges at an attractive girl seated on a folding chair. She looked about quickly before producing a piece of paper and asking the boys for their autographs. Jake laughed, but Peter whipped out a pen and signed, leaning close to her as he did so.

Jake rolled his eyes and marched through the doorway. Whoa. He couldn't believe the lights. Lights were everywhere, hung from stands that reached higher than the decks on the bowls, and planted everywhere along the street section. He shaded his eyes with his arm. The place was as hot as a sauna, and workers were still setting up lights. He gripped his board nervously. How'd he get himself into this? What was Marco going to ask of them? What if he couldn't do the tricks he was ordered to do?

"Jake."

He turned to see Aaron beside him. Black hat,

black T-shirt, black pants, identification badge around his neck. Jake wondered if Aaron had any clothes that weren't black. The skater wasn't smiling, but that was hardly new.

"Hi, Aaron. Crazy in here, isn't it?"

"Totally."

Silence hung between them. What is it Jake expected Aaron to say, anyway? "Congratulations?" "Awesome second heat at the tryouts?" Or "Hand it over right now. You know you're a poser and the role should have been mine."

"It's going to be hot skating under these lights." Jake couldn't think of anything else to say.

"Everyone should have that kind of problem," Aaron replied with no hint of humor.

"Hey, Aaron. Good to see you," Peter spoke up from behind. "Hope you get to skate today, too. This is pretty strange, isn't it? Where's Kwasi?"

"Under the ramps with Billy. Doing the rehab training thing. The guy's useless. Don't know why he bothers."

Jake wondered whether Aaron meant Kwasi or Billy was useless. It occurred to him that at times, he preferred Billy to Aaron.

"Boys, right on time. Excellent," Marco said as he approached with hand held out. Peter and Jake each shook his hand. Aaron just looked at Marco.

"So, we'll be ready for you in about ten. Feel free to warm up on the half-pipe. All three of you," he added, as if feeling the intensity of Aaron's stare. "Then, I'll explain what tricks you'll be doing, and my production assistant, Miranda" — he nodded at a young woman hovering nearby — "will take Jake and Peter to the costume and makeup trailers while the cameramen and safety people finish setting up. Aaron, there's coffee and snacks outside the front door while you're hanging around. But first, let me introduce the three of you to the cast Jake and Peter are playing." He signaled two boys conferring with a man holding a clipboard. They ambled over.

"Boys, this is Aydin, who Peter will be representing." Jake peered at Aydin, who was roughly the same age, height, and weight as Peter, and had curly hair, but otherwise bore no resemblance to his buddy. In fact, his hair was black. Jake wondered if Marco's staff was going to make Peter dye his hair. Aydin nodded curtly and looked Peter up and down.

"And this is Karl, Jake's double."

Jake turned his eyes on Karl. He looked about fifteen, like Jake, and had dark brown hair, the same build as Jake, and a face that made Jake feel as if he was looking in a mirror. Karl grinned and held out his hand.

"Everyone's been telling me they found me the perfect double. I didn't believe it, but here we are.

Maybe we have a relative in common somewhere back on the family tree."

Jake's tongue felt thick in his mouth. He cast about for something polite and intelligent to say, but nothing came out. He just nodded dumbly and finally looked away. So this was why Marco had been staring at him. Jake's awkwardness prompted Marco to chuckle. One by one, the other boys joined in the laughter. Jake snatched a glance at Karl again, saw that his eyes were friendly.

"Nice to meet you," Jake finally said. "I guess I know now how I got the part."

"I'm Aaron," Aaron declared, stepping forward. "The alternate."

"Nice to meet you, Aaron," Karl said.

Aydin mumbled "Same," but his eyes were flashing about the room as if he were bored.

"Well, boys — stuntboys, that is — I'll turn you over to Miranda. I'm needed to check out camera positions." Marco and the actors strode away, followed by several people at their heels, all trying to talk to Marco at once.

The next hour passed in a blur. Jake, Peter, and Aaron warmed up on the street section, which didn't feel familiar at all under the glare of the lights and the stare of the workers. Then they followed Miranda to a trailer where a man with more earrings than ears shoved clothing at them until they were both outfitted in clothing that matched the shorts and T-shirts Karl and Aydin had been wearing. Miranda then hustled them to the makeup trailer, where Jake endured getting his face powdered — "to keep your skin from looking shiny in the lights," someone explained — and Peter was rendered speechless by orders to wear a wig of dark curls under his skateboard helmet.

Back on the ramps, Peter managed to cut Aaron's guffaws short by saying, "This'll be your wig if I get banged up."

When Marco appeared at Jake's and Peter's sides, the buzz of conversation in the background dimmed to whispers. "We're going to block the action," he ordered.

"That means we're rehearsing with the cameras on their dollies so we can decide if the lights need adjusting," Miranda explained to them quietly.

Jake glanced at the camera-holding dollies, which resembled something between oversized children's tricycles and robots on tripods. Like miniature railway cars, these metal contraptions moved on grooved wheels that fit into tracks the staff were continually taking apart, moving, and putting back together again. This way, they could run alongside the skateboarders, shooting them on the run.

"Peter, I need a boardslide."

"Okay, that's good. Jake, go for a 360-flip on the funbox please, and make it a high one."

Though he tried not to let the movie-shoot equipment distract him, Jake was fascinated by the toy-sized, camera-equipped, remote-control helicopters providing aerial views of the boys' stunts. Lucky crewmembers who spend all day pushing the buttons directing those, he thought. Except for the cameras on them, the helicopters were just like the remote-controlled flying toys he'd seen in public parks.

Besides the dollies and helicopters, the room was also filled with small cranes holding cameras whose cables stretched down to a monitor on a three-legged stand, in front of which Marco sat.

"Honey wagon break," someone called out after a while.

Jake looked at Peter, half expecting a wagon filled with honey-laden biscuits to roll onto the skatepark floor. As if reading his mind, Miranda appeared with the hint of a smile and said, "He means a bathroom break. We call the trailer full of toilet units the honey wagon."

After an hour of action, during which Jake's nerves were as on edge as they'd ever been, the boys were exhausted. Jake had managed to produce all the tricks requested of him on demand, even if with occasional difficulty.

"Cut and print!" Marco finally shouted. "Not bad,

boys. Quick snack break, then I want Jake to re-do that benihana. Peter, you're done, but stick around in case I change my mind. After Jake's reshoot, you two are free. See you back here tomorrow noon for Shoot No. 2. That goes for you too, Aaron, of course."

Jake was almost too tired to make his way to the food table, where smiling caterers oversaw line-ups of crew members pile paper plates high with wraps, fresh fruit, a choice of gourmet salads, and dessert bars.

"I'm in heaven," Peter moaned as he steered his plate to a folding chair in the sunshine outside.

"I'm totally wiped," Jake said, dropping into a chair beside Peter, who'd shed his wig for the moment. Jake wondered how he was going to lift himself out of his chair ever again.

"I'm bored," Aaron said, sucking on a chocolate-covered strawberry before taking a seat beside them.

"Do we get seconds for free?" Peter wondered.

"All the helpings you need," Karl said, plopping down across from them. "You're burning more calories than anyone here."

"Can you skate?" Jake asked, curious.

"If you can call it that," Karl said with a chuckle. "Let's just say I can stay on the board long enough for the close-up shots needed. Better you than me on the dangerous work."

"Can Marco skate?" Aaron asked.

"He can, for sure," Karl replied, turning to study Aaron briefly. "Not that I'm an expert on whether he'd impress a pro."

"Is Kwasi going to be helping on the skating scenes?" Peter asked Karl.

"Who's Kwasi?"

"The skatepark manager."

"Oh, the hyper dude with dreadlocks hanging out under the floor with that retard? Don't think so. How come he has to keep crawling under the, um, the ..."

"Ramps," Jake offered. "Screws and boards can work their way loose even after a short sesh — I mean session. Can't have boards falling off during skating, or someone can get hurt. They need to be inspected and tightened constantly."

"Wow. Didn't know skateparks were so high main-tenance. Kind of like my girlfriend," he joked, then hopped up and sauntered off toward Aydin, who was busy signing autographs for a crowd of local boys on the other side of their roped-off area.

"Well, I hear those desserts calling my name again," Peter announced, standing up and stretching.

"And I see Alyson," Jake said. He turned, but Aaron's chair was empty. No big deal. Poor guy. Jake would be bored as an alternate, too. Jake rose and made his way to the rope fence to give Alyson a hug. He blinked when he noticed a woman with a camera shooting them.

"That your sweetie, stuntboy?" the photographer asked. She wore a badge that said "*Chilliwack Times.*"

"This is my sister," Jake returned slowly.

"I'll see you later," Alyson said to Jake as the photographer moved her way with a notebook and pen. "Marco is trying to get your attention."

The supper had revived Jake, but it also sat a little heavily in his stomach. And Marco seemed to be harder to please after the break. He kept having Jake demonstrate moves again and again. Finally, he seemed satisfied enough to order the cameras to roll. But as Jake hopped on his board and began rolling toward the lip, Billy appeared, walking firmly across the floor toward Jake.

"Cut! Get that boy off the set!" Marco shouted. But Billy ignored Marco. He walked right up to Jake, who had stepped off his board.

"Jake," Billy whispered, pressing two screws into Jake's hand. "Someone's been messing with the constructions. Give me five to make sure you're okay. Keep 'em, I got lotsa screws."

"I said, get him out of here," Marco shouted again. "Where's Kwasi?"

Jake pocketed the screws, a little stunned.

Kwasi appeared. "I'm here, Marco. Billy, what's up?"

Billy, looking relieved to be rescued by Kwasi, walked briskly to his boss and said a few words. Kwasi nodded and said, "Sorry, Marco. Need five minutes for technical adjustments."

Marco looked cross, but shouted, "Everybody back to first positions in five."

Minutes later, Kwasi appeared and gave Marco a thumbs up. Marco nodded at Jake, who resumed his position and began pumping in the bowl. Soon, he flew up over the lip and popped an ollie high enough to kick out his back foot. With his forward foot still touching the near-vertical board as if an invisible hinge connected the two, he kicked out his back leg so far that he felt like a gymnast doing the splits. Now he caught the board's tail with his opposite hand, then extended his front foot and landed neatly. He smiled inwardly. Marco would be happy with that one, he was certain. It felt way cleaner, way sicker than his morning's attempt.

"It's a wrap for the day!" Marco shouted with enthusiasm. "Way to go, Jake."

Jake looked around, caught Aaron's dark eyes watching from a corner of the vert ramp. He imagined the *Chilliwack Times* photographer aiming her camera at him that moment. Her lens would have shattered from the spite on Aaron's face.

He turned to Peter, who was hurtling toward him, hand raised to slap him hard on the back. "Way to show us how a benihana is done, old buddy. You're the man."

Jake smiled. *I'm the man,* he thought. But as he stuffed his hands in his shorts pockets on the way to the costume trailer, he touched the cold metal of the screws.

Billy's not all there, he reminded himself. And screws work their way loose all the time.

12   Midnight Skate

T he old wooden window in Jake's bed-
room squeaked just a little as the boys raised it slowly.
Peter looked behind and listened carefully as he raised
a foot to the ledge, ready to exit. No one had heard
them. And it had stopped raining. Perfect.

One by one, the boys dropped to the grass in the
backyard, boards in hand. It still smelled freshly
mowed, hours after he and Jake had run the hand
mower around it while telling Alyson and Jake's mom
all about their first day on the movie set. Sandra and
Alyson had roared when they'd heard about Peter's wig.

Peter shivered a little as he and his buddy stood
there in the dark.

"I think we'll be glad for our fleeces tonight," he
whispered to Jake as they moved through the back gate.

"Maybe," Jake responded, "but you might regret
wearing a red one when the moon comes out."

Peter glanced up, saw that the full moon was going to play hide-and-seek with clouds all night. Yes, black like Jake's would have been better. Then again, hopefully they wouldn't get themselves into a situation where they had to run and hide.

It took less than ten minutes to reach Sk8. There, one solitary light shone from the roof, illuminating Bruce, Aaron, and Gabe pressing their ears against the locked doors.

"What's up?" Peter asked. They moved to make room for him. He plastered his ear against the cold metal and heard the rumble and clatter of a skateboard in high-action mode. He raised an eyebrow and checked his watch. "Who's in there at this hour?"

"Kwasi," Aaron said with a smile. "It's his secret workout time. Too bad there are no windows or peepholes."

Peter agreed. The boys moved into the shadows just beyond the pool of light. Judging from their outfits, either Aaron had dressed them or they were headed for a funeral: All were wearing black.

"Let's go," Aaron said, disappearing into the night with the tip of his board pinched firmly in one hand. Peter accelerated to match Aaron's long strides. Jake fell in with Gabe and Bruce behind.

"So the BMXers have taken over the outdoor plaza, have you noticed?" Aaron said at length, voice low.

"No, haven't seen them. Does Kwasi know?"

"Yes, and he's letting them because they're friends of Alyson's, I hear."

"They are *not* friends of Alyson's. Jake has warned her to keep away from them."

Aaron slowed and looked at Peter. In the dim moonlight, Peter caught an amused sneer on his lips. "That makes Jake a bad dad, 'cause little sis has been biking up a storm there, sucking up to anyone who'll step off their bike and loan it to her for a minute, including Billy."

"Billy?"

"Yes, our Billy. He used to ride, you know. Now when he can break free of Kwasi, he farts around the outdoor bowl like a crappy jock, but Alyson thinks he's good. But he's smart enough to disappear fast when the BMX gang shows."

"Shhh. Jake's not far behind us. Let me break this to him, okay?"

"Whatever you say, Peter. Alyson's okay, you know. She seems pretty chill for a kid."

"I said shhh."

By now, Peter had lost any sense of where they were going. He hoped Jake knew where they were in case they got separated from Aaron and company. He was relieved when, after a twenty-minute trek through back streets and brush, they finally slowed by an industrial park where a floodlight lit up a yard paved with concrete and filled with equipment strewn about. Peter blinked and the equipment transformed itself into appealing obstacles. A wide board half fallen from a rusty fence presented a perfect ramp. A trio of six-foot-tall metal full pipes invited some sick vert moves, and best of all, a railing ran all around one edge of a concrete loading dock.

"Gabe's on watch first," Aaron declared in a hushed voice. "If anyone comes, he whistles, we separate, and meet back behind Sk8."

Peter nodded, saw Jake do the same. He was glad he and Jake had snatched two hours of sleep before they'd snuck out tonight. Even though they'd skated less than five hours during the shoot today, they'd both been bushed. The strain of performing tricks on command had drained him more than he'd imagined. But he'd loved how Marco had been impressed by his tricks. The director had ordered hardly any retakes on his stuff. He'd also loved meeting Aydin and Karl. That would be him some time in the future: an actor being nice to newly hired stuntboys and offering up autographs to the kids gathered at the rope. No, take that back. Peter would be an actor who insisted on doing his own stunts.

The only thing Peter couldn't figure out was why Jake had been so quiet after the sesh. It had gone fine for him. Marco had had to goad him a little more than Peter, and had taken extra time to reshoot the last trick, but Jake had done competent moves, and Marco had seemed satisfied. In fact, for Jake's level of ability, he'd shone. But Jake had been really quiet since the shoot, stewing over something — nothing that he'd share with Peter. Peter hoped he wasn't going into one of his dad funks again.

Aaron, always head of the pack, was the first to skate. He rolled up a ramp onto the loading dock and cruised halfway along it before lifting effortlessly up onto a rail, where he did the world's longest grind before sailing off and disappearing amidst the field of obstacles. Bruce, body bent like a sailboat tacking in a windstorm, roared up and down the insides of the full pipes, pulling off some eye-popping carves. The noise of their wheels in the still night was sure to draw somebody — if anybody was within a mile — but Peter figured that was unlikely. Peter and Jake moved forward like a team, winding and pumping and grinding as smiles grew on their faces. Peter glanced up once at the corner of the warehouse, where Gabe stood sentry, his wiry body pressed against a dark wall. After twenty minutes of wicked fun, Aaron silently replaced Gabe, who joined the party, screeching down rail after rail like he was programmed to be in a video game.

Peter bailed off his board on an attempted frontside blunt.

"Lame," Aaron called down in a hushed tone.

"He's just jerkin' you around," Bruce said quietly as the two found themselves in one of the pipes.

"Why do you hang with him?" Peter dared to ask.

Bruce shrugged, kept skating. The two were drawing figure eights inside the pipe when they heard Aaron's whistle. Peter nearly slammed from stopping too fast inside the pipe as he stepped off his board and grabbed it to run. Police car headlights illuminated the yard with the force of movie spotlights. As Peter did a fifty-yard dash to the darkest ditch he could sight, a police officer gave chase. *Oh, man, this was bad. How'd the cops get here so fast?* Aaron hadn't given the skaters enough time.

Peter, with no idea where the rest of the guys were, tripped and fell headlong into the ditch, which was filled with rank water. He heard twigs crack behind him, saw a figure standing over him.

I've been had, Peter thought as he gulped and looked up into the shadowy face of the police officer just before he was blinded by the beam of a flashlight on his face. *I'm in major trouble now. Major. I hope the rest of the guys get away.* He raised his arm and let the officer pull him out of the watery ditch. The tug was none too gentle.

13   The Kickflip Indy

The movie lights were making Jake's head pound. He popped his third aspirin of the day and stepped on his board. He spent most of his mandatory warm-up time rocking it back and forth. He couldn't believe the mess he was in. And he could barely bring himself to look at his new stuntboy partner, Aaron.

The police hadn't been one bit persuaded by Marco that they should change Peter's one o'clock grilling down at the station. Especially since they'd managed to reach Richard and Laura Montpetit for a simultaneous telephone conference.

Marco hadn't been willing to change his shoot time, so Aaron had been promoted, at least for the day. Jake rocked his board harder. He was operating on almost zero sleep, had no idea how he was going to get through the day's paces. He wondered how much sleep Aaron had had. The four had waited awhile at

Sk8 for Peter before breaking up and going home. That's when Jake had faced the wrath of his mother, who'd been awakened by officers in a squad car returning Peter.

Peter and Jake had commiserated all night. Both were going to be grounded now for what might as well be forever. Why? Just because they'd been having a little clean fun on the town? How could their boards possibly damage a couple of rusty pipes and railings in an industrial park? Okay, so they'd been trespassing. But it wasn't like they were out to steal or damage property or do drugs. Didn't the police have more serious crimes to chase?

Jake sighed. Yes, it had occurred to him that Aaron may have planned this all along. He'd been on watch when the police had moved in. Had he purposely delayed the signal? Then again, Peter had been wearing that bright red fleece, or maybe just gotten unlucky. Any of the guys could have gotten caught, Jake figured. Just because Peter's rotten luck had ended up getting Aaron the stuntboy gig didn't mean Aaron had set it all up.

"Jake, wake up." Jake heard the irritation in Marco's tone and shook himself. "I said, it's time to check in with costume and makeup."

Jake nodded and followed Aaron. He tried not to smile when Aaron got fitted with the wig. Aaron's brown hair no more resembled Aydin's than Peter's blond curls. His feet felt like lead as he followed Aaron from the trailers back into the park. It seemed easier to follow than lead Aaron. Jake was in such a fog, he nearly slammed into someone wheeling a dolly of soft drink boxes from a truck to the catering table.

"Hey, watch where you're going, stuntboy," the delivery boy said.

Jake blinked. He knew that voice. He squinted at the boy's ID badge, then at his face. Judd gave Jake a sardonic smirk before moving on.

As Marco barked out orders, Jake struggled to keep up. The tricks Marco wanted today were more diffi-cult, and they'd have been tough to pull off even on one of Jake's better days. He wished Peter were there to encourage him. A couple of times, he looked out over the milling crew for Kwasi. He took some encourage-ment from Kwasi's sympathetic eyes. At the same time, it dawned on him that Billy wasn't with Kwasi, that he hadn't seen Billy all day. Where was Billy?

At break, he was careful not to eat too much, for fear it would make him even dozier. He managed to escape to Kwasi's office.

"Hey, Kwasi, how's it going?"

"Fine, better than for you, from what I hear of events last night."

"Yeah. Where's Billy?"

Kwasi lowered his head. "Fired."

"Fired? You fired him? Why?"

"Marco made me. Because he keeps arriving late, and because he disrupted things a little yesterday."

"How is calling time out to replace screws for safety reasons disrupting things?"

"I know. I agree. But Marco is my boss during the shoot, and I guess Billy should have spoken to me instead of walking across the set to talk to you. Anyway, there have been other problems with Billy."

"Like him biking on work time out front with Alyson? Peter told me. I wish you'd told me earlier. Still seems like he should have had a second chance."

"It wasn't my decision to fire him, Jake."

"Maybe you should have stood up to Marco."

"Jake, you tend to your business, and I'll tend to mine, okay?"

"Sorry, Kwasi." Jake lifted his board wearily and tucked it under his arm. "I wish Marco would let you coach me. I'm having a rough time today."

"I already asked Marco. He said no. You'll get through it, Jake. Chin up."

Chin up. That wasn't psychobabble or coach-speak.

But Jake knew he had to stop looking for someone to help him. He had to buck up on his own, he decided. *Okay, this is hard, but hundreds of guys would love to be in my shoes. Life's not so bad. In fact, life is good. Keep telling yourself that: Life is good.*

Jake walked more confidently back to the bench beside Aaron, awaiting Marco's call. *Marco,* he thought. So Marco had forced Kwasi to fire Billy, and Billy may or may not have saved Jake from an accident yesterday. And Marco wouldn't let Kwasi coach Jake because it might cost him a dime.

Forget that. Life is good. Buck up.

"Jake," Marco said. "I want you and Aaron to work the street section in perfect synch today. Follow his tricks, hitting the same obstacles, height, and body language move for move. Keep just a few paces behind whatever he does. He's leader."

Jake nodded. Aaron was going to have a field day with this one. He was going to make Jake pay for the evil of having one-upped him at tryouts. Well, Jake wasn't going to let him; Jake was determined to keep up if it killed him.

For the next hour without breaks, Aaron concocted a punishing routine. Jake, streaming sweat from every pore, kept up, but only barely. Marco nodded approvingly. But Jake knew it wouldn't last. As Aaron began pushing the envelope of his own abilities, Jake began bailing.

"Cut! Jake, pull yourself together. We're wasting film."

Jake tried. He tried with everything he had. But Aaron was the better skater, there was no way around that, and Aaron had an agenda. Why didn't Marco tell Aaron to tone it down? If he wanted the two of them skating neck and neck, he needed to take some pressure off Jake.

"Cut! Jake, this isn't working. Everyone take five."

Jake waited for Marco to come give him a lecture. But when he had the nerve to look up, Marco had disappeared. Instead, Miranda was standing there. Her voice was gentle.

"Cup of coffee, Jake? I'll walk you outside to the refreshment table."

Jake followed her, grateful for the show of sympathy, even if she did get called away as soon as they reached the catering table. He poured extra sugar into his coffee and nabbed a muffin. He watched Aaron sign autographs at the rope.

Kwasi appeared at his elbow. "Jake, Marco has given Aaron an hour off." The manager stirred mounds of sugar into his coffee. "That's good news, don't you think?"

"I guess," Jake said. But could he please Marco's demands even without Aaron setting the pace?

"And you know what? I get a new rehab tomorrow morning," Kwasi said.

"Yeah? That's good for you. So how did this one get to be a rehab?"

"He got hit by a car while hitchhiking. Flew threw the air. Has retrograde amnesia."

"That's gruesome, Kwasi. You're supposed to be cheering me up on my coffee break," Jake teased. "And you're doing the big words again."

"Sorry, Jake. Hit it up after the break and you'll be done for the day."

"Done for the day sounds good, Kwasi." Jake looked up in time to see Miranda walking toward him. He made himself smile, which actually felt good. He picked up his board and followed her.

"Jake, can you do a kickflip Indy?" Marco pressed him as soon as he entered the building.

Jake looked over to the bowls, felt his heart begin to pound. Should he tell Marco the truth? Did he have a choice?

"Um, I'm a little sketch on that one, Marco. I might need some coaching."

"You lead in with a backside air, then you kickflip. You have to grab when you can. Ready to give it a try?" Marco was leaning way too close to Jake, and his tone was two shades away from threatening.

"You might do better having Aaron perform that one," Jake said, as boldly as he dared.

Marco looked startled that anyone would defy him. Then he seemed to catch himself. He smiled.

"Ahhh, perhaps, but the cameras are going to be

just close up enough on this one that we need it to be Karl's best double."

"Okay." Jake straightened his shoulders and gave Marco a grin. "On the double!" Or should he have said "double trouble" Jake wondered, searching for some humor in the situation. Hey, what was the worst that could happen? He'd bail or slam. Marco would get mad. Marco would fire him. Jake would still get paid for two out of three days' work. *I can only do what I can do*, Jake thought. He'd give it his best shot, even if he'd never successfully done a kick-flip Indy before.

"Camera, sound!" Marco shouted.

"Rolling," a cameraman reported.

"Speed," the sound woman shouted.

Jake was disappointed not to see someone leap out of a director's chair and hold up a chalkboard, then clap hinged, striped yardsticks together with a bang. Instead, he noted, a digital screen that resembled a quartz clock radio declared the movie's title and what section was being filmed.

Jake started from the line Marco had indicated and sped toward the bowls at the highest speed he could muster. He kickflipped and grabbed. But just as he was about to leap to the deck, he stopped dead, seized by panic. He cursed and swung around to return to his starting line, wincing in anticipation of Marco's wrath. Before he got there, Kwasi appeared in front of him with a helmet on.

"Jake, watch me, and watch me close. I know you can do it if you focus on how I ollie out."

Before Jake could say anything, Kwasi had grabbed his board and positioned himself on the starting line. Jake drew back, relieved to get some coaching, even as he heard Marco on the mike: "Kwasi. Get out of there. No one asked you to help."

Kwasi shot for the bowls like a bullet, his body and board flowing so smoothly that Jake gaped. He was a pro, no question. He was amazing. *Focus on how I ollie out.* Jake latched his eyes on Kwasi's feet and held his breath as Kwasi sucked up his board and sprang to the deck. That's where he would have landed, but with an ear-splitting crack, the deck caved in, and Kwasi disappeared from view.

Jake was part of the crush of people who surged forward, horrified. A safety crew member clambered up and dropped down the hole, while others quickly formed a line to keep people from pressing too close or collapsing the construction further. The man who'd dropped nimbly down the gap popped his head up and said, "Call an ambulance."

Jake, seeing he wasn't going to get near Kwasi the way most people were pushing, ran against the flow to where he and Alyson had entered the undersides of the bowls earlier. Grabbing the flashlight from its hook, he crawled to where he could see Kwasi's feet.

"Hey, kid, out of here. Leave this to emergency personnel," the crew member warned. But Jake was already by Kwasi's side.

"Kwasi?" He put his hand on Kwasi's forehead, but the man was unconscious. Gently, Jake drew some braids away from Kwasi's face and reached beside him to pull one of Gabe's blankets over his chest. "You'll be okay," he promised, voice cracking.

As a stretcher was lowered from above, Jake studied the support beams beneath the deck. He counted one, two, three missing. No wonder half the deck had given way. He stood, shaking, and flicked on his flashlight. Screws that Kwasi himself would have tightened before the last coffee break were a thread away from falling out. Jake's flashlight beam located the missing supports propped neatly near Gabe's bed.

Someone's been messing with the constructions, Billy had said.

Jake dove for Gabe's second blanket, wrapped it around the three boards, and crawled with them back the way he'd come, stashing the boards where no one was likely to find them — fingerprints intact, he hoped.

Then he popped back up the other side and watched ambulance attendants lift Kwasi's stretcher and take it away. Jake scanned the room for Aaron, found him at the opposite end of the park staring at Jake. Their eyes locked, but all Jake could read was anger. Anger at who? And why?

Jake looked down and saw that his hands were shaking. *That could have been me,* he recognized for the first time. *That would have been me if I'd finished the jump to the deck. Who removed the boards, and was the accident meant for me?*

He shuddered and felt a chill enter his body. Kwasi, unconscious. Is that how it had been for Lex and Billy? Healthy, lively people one minute, then — wham — unconscious and facing a long, slow climb to the status of floor-mopping rehabs. For the first time, Jake tried to imagine Lex and Billy as people without memory problems, people he might hang out and laugh with. For a second, he burned with shame at how he had let them spook him, at how uncomfortable he had always been around "mentals." Alyson had come around to accepting Billy as he was.

"Attention, everyone." Marco was on the mike. "Today's shoot has been cancelled. Please return here at noon tomorrow for the last and final shoot. Everyone but safety and maintenance crew is dismissed. Thank you for staying calm during this unfortunate accident."

Accident, Jake thought bitterly, looking around again for Aaron, but not seeing him. Accident it was not.

14   Garage Clash

Peter wasn't home yet. That worried Jake. He had to be finished at the police station. He must have stopped somewhere for a sandwich. Jake found Alyson in his bedroom on the computer.

"Hi, Jake, how did it go today?"

"Don't want to talk about it." Actually, he did, but there was the faint possibility that Judd was involved, and Jake didn't want to get into a discussion on that with Alyson right now. He wanted privacy to phone the hospital to see how Kwasi was.

"Uh-oh. That doesn't sound good. Peter called. Said he'd be here soon."

"Thanks. Do you mind if I have my room to myself?"

"Awww, please Jake. I'm finding important stuff on the Net."

Jake, so tired he could barely stay upright, propelled

himself toward the screen, hoping that if he showed interest for a minute, she might clear out.

"A BMX site. How is that important?"

"Look at these pedals for sale."

"BMX pedals. Who cares? You don't have a bike to buy pedals for, and Mom's in no position to buy one for you, if that's what you're thinking."

"Plastic pedals, Jake. Special pedals and pegs that let BMX bikes perform in indoor skateparks without damaging the surface. Kwasi said if I could find some, and Judd and his friends would buy them, he'd let them into the skatepark."

Jake shook his head. "Alyson, trust me, that's not high priority right now. Can you please leave me alone for awhile?"

"But it is important," she pushed. "Judd said he'd make trouble for Kwasi if Kwasi didn't let them in."

Jake's head lifted. "Trouble?"

"You know, give him a hard time." Her expression was pained, like she didn't know whose side she was on. Then again, if she was researching pedals and pegs on the Net, she did know whose side she was on. Jake felt his pulse quicken.

A part of him knew that it was no big deal Alyson had a sort-of crush on an older boy, even one that Jake didn't approve of. But her comment about Judd threatening to make trouble for Kwasi, given what had just occurred, called for some thinking time. Jake patted Alyson's head as he headed for the one place that always allowed him to think clearly: the garage. The place where his dad had always been to comfort him. He grabbed the phone on the way and dialed the hospital.

"Are you a relative of Kwasi Kumar?" an emergency-room attendant asked suspiciously after he'd been put on hold by several people.

"No."

"Then I'm sorry, but we can't release any information at this point," she said sternly.

He let himself into the garage, put his back against the closed door, and slumped to the cold concrete. He needed more aspirin. He needed sleep. He needed to know Kwasi was going to be okay. He looked across the room, saw the two halves of the quarter-pipe his dad had made all those years ago. He rose, walked over, pushed them together, and lay down in the middle as if it were a bed. He curled up, wrapped his arms around himself, and closed his eyes. He let the years fall away, tried to be seven again. He waited for his father to enter the garage.

The door burst open. Jake sat up.

"So, you sure have a lot to answer for." Aaron was towering over him, flanked by Bruce and Gabe, whose faces were as hostile as on the first day Jake and Peter had encountered them at the outdoor plaza.

"Huh?" Jake wasn't sure if he'd fallen asleep, but he could hardly believe these guys were invading his refuge.

"First you get Billy fired so he can't catch you sneaking under the constructions. Then you take support boards away, wrap them in a blanket, and hide them in a far corner where you think no one will find them. Then you refuse to do a trick Marco asks you to, 'cause you've set it all up for me to have an accident. You even tell Marco I should do it instead of you. And now Kwasi's in the hospital."

Jake felt like he'd been hit with a bowling ball. *Aaron* was accusing *him* of sabotage?

"Or was your prank aimed at the BMXers? Gabe here overheard them threatening Kwasi if Kwasi didn't give them indoor skatepark time. Maybe Alyson had a line on them trying to crash the movie set today, and you thought you'd arrange a little surprise for them this time? Who was the accident aimed at, Jake: me or the BMXers? Or do you have something against Kwasi that I don't know about?"

Jake struggled to his feet and struggled for words.

"*Me* cause an accident? You think I removed the boards? I was the one who got under there in time to see that they'd been messed with, while Kwasi was lying there. Someone took out boards *and* loosened screws right before my session. If you touched those boards that I wrapped up and hid, you've messed with the fingerprints I was trying to save. Could that be because they would have been yours, Aaron?"

Jake was wide awake now and shaking with anger. It didn't matter that there were three against one. He was ready to go down fighting.

Aaron's hands rolled up into fists and he took a step toward Jake.

"I don't have to mess with boards or make someone go down. No one was re-shooting me, because I do things right the first time. You're the one who's into building constructions. Everyone knows that. You're the one who would know exactly how to set up a fall like that. And everyone knows you hated Billy. You hated all the retards, but especially the one teaching your kid sister how to bike. You figured you could weaken the deck while Kwasi was looking the other way, but not if Billy was around, too."

Jake took a step forward, eyes flashing. "Marco made Kwasi fire Billy for showing up late and playing around outside on work time. I would never have gotten Billy fired. It was Billy who saved my butt yesterday. Or are you going to deny that you loosened some screws yesterday, too?"

Jake fished in his pocket, found the screws still there, produced them while watching Aaron's face. Aaron stared at them, uncomprehending. "That's why

Billy called a time out yesterday," Jake continued, voice rising to a shout. "He knew it was dangerous. He tried to warn me someone had been down there. If I'd listened to him, maybe Kwasi wouldn't be injured. But you, or was it Gabe" — Jake turned on Gabe — "snuck in there and took the boards out after Kwasi had done a check on the lunch hour. Then *you* dare to accuse *me*?" He paused to grab a breath. "I guess as they say, a good offense is the best defense. Throws people off your own scent. But that's not going to work, Aaron."

"If screws were messed with yesterday, it wasn't me, you useless poser," Aaron said, drawing his arm back to let fly. Jake felt the fist connect with his stomach, but not hard enough to take his breath away. He looked around the garage for something to use in his defense.

"It was you or Gabe," Jake said, picking up a broken broom handle and looking from one to the other. "I know all about Gabe's little hideaway, and how he sneaks in through the ventilation system. You know those undersides real well, Gabe, don't you, and you always do what Aaron says."

"I didn't remove any boards, and I don't have to use the ventilation system anymore, because Kwasi gave me keys," Gabe said, eyes narrowed, voice steady. "I could care less who is playing stuntboy, and I don't take orders from anyone, including Aaron. I haven't been near Sk8 since we met there last night," he finished.

Had that been only last night? Jake wondered. The five of them, playing at midnight together like friends? He caught the movement of someone listening outside the garage door and recognized Peter's shoes. The other three boys didn't know he was there.

"Try and tell me you didn't set up last night to get rid of Peter," Jake continued, feeling bold now that he had a broom handle in his hand and his buddy as backup. He was speaking to anyone who cared to answer his challenge. *It was his garage. How dare they.*

"You think we set up Peter to get picked up?" Bruce spoke up for the first time. "Give me a break. Like we'd take the chance of getting picked up ourselves. Like we'd be able to guess the police would want him the exact hour the shoot was going to happen the next day. Get real, Jake. We invited you along 'cause we were starting to think you were okay."

Jake lowered his broom handle a few inches. He eyed Aaron warily.

"I did not set myself up for an accident," Jake declared slowly, deliberately injecting sarcasm into his tone. "I chickened out on the first run-up to the deck because I'd never done a kickflip Indy. I don't have to tell you I'm not as good a skater as Aaron, but I was trying. I told Marco that Aaron should do it instead of me so he'd get the shot he wanted, but he wouldn't listen. I'd have been up on that deck my second run if

Kwasi hadn't cut in. That means *I'd* have been in the hospital. And maybe I'd have been injured the day before, if Billy hadn't spotted the screws. Someone seems to be aiming at me."

He let the logic of that sink in.

"It wasn't Gabe or me," Aaron returned forcefully. "I won't pretend I wasn't half hoping something would happen to you or Peter to let me get some action, but I didn't set anything up. Not at the industrial park, and not today. And I sure never asked Gabe to mess with the ramp. Skaters don't hurt skaters," he declared.

Jake eyed Aaron's fists. Aaron lowered them.

"So maybe it was the BMX guys," Bruce suggested.

"Are you sure the boards under the deck didn't just fall down?" Everyone turned as Peter entered the garage. Aaron, Bruce, and Gabe looked a little stricken that he'd clearly been listening for a while.

"They were propped against Gabe's bed," Jake said, regretting his choice of words as he saw Gabe's face redden and his eyes study the floor.

"Then we're really going to have to watch our backs tomorrow on the last shoot," Peter said. "If someone's out to injure us, they have one more shot. Will you guys help us?"

Aaron, Bruce, and Gabe nodded, faces long.

Aaron coughed. "Uh, sorry, Jake. Guess we kind of busted in here without having our info straight."

You sure did, Jake thought. He shrugged. "Guess I said some stupid stuff, too." He turned to Peter. "How'd it go down at the station?"

"Lots of pressure to name names, but I don't break," his buddy responded with a tired smile. "I'm up to my you-know-what in alligators at home, but let's not change the subject. We need to organize our own safety system for tomorrow."

"And someone has to pay for hurting Kwasi," Aaron declared.

"Gabe and I don't have ID to get onto the set," Bruce reminded them.

"Shhh. That's my mom's car pulling up," Jake said. "Let's meet at Sk8 nine o'clock tomorrow to figure this out."

"We're practiced at scattering," Bruce whispered. "You and Peter need to walk out of here real casually."

As Jake and Peter sauntered out of the garage, Jake noticed the boys' three skateboards leaning against the outside wall. Maybe his mom wouldn't notice them.

She ran into the backyard and slung her arms around him. "Jake, I heard what happened at the skatepark. I was so frightened you might have gotten hurt, too."

"I'm okay, Mom." He didn't wriggle out of her embrace. Finally, she released him. "Hi, Peter." She straightened herself, took a deep breath. "I just came back from an errand at the hospital. Your friend Kwasi's in Emergency, you know."

"How is he?" Jake spoke up.

"He regained consciousness in the ambulance and is getting tested for brain damage on a CAT scan. He'll be kept for observation overnight."

"That sounds hopeful," Jake said, chest tightening at the phrase "brain damage."

"Aaron, Bruce, and Gabe — did I get all those names right? — you can come out of the garage now, because I have a message for Gabe from Kwasi," she said.

Jake and Peter looked at her, then at each other. Three boys filed slowly out of the garage.

"Hi, I'm Sandra, Jake's mom."

"Hello," they mumbled in chorus, feet shuffling. Jake wasn't sure how this was going to play out. He was pretty sure that "grounded" didn't include plotting with skaters in the garage.

"Which one is Gabe?"

Gabe's eyes darted every which way before he stepped forward.

"Kwasi asked me to ask you if you could do all the skatepark maintenance tomorrow. He said you have a key and know how. He'll let Marco know that you and Bruce are in charge."

Gabe's normally expressionless face brightened. "Yeah, okay."

"He said you need to be there at nine to meet and train a new TBI." She looked at Gabe suspiciously. "What's a TBI?"

Gabe looked confused for a minute.

"Traumatic brain injury," Jake reminded him. "A rehab."

"Oh. Sure," Gabe said, eyes on his feet.

"So Kwasi's talking?" Peter queried.

"Talking, giving orders, asking about you guys, phoning Marco, and doing everything but skateboarding around the emergency room," she said, hands on her hips.

"Can we go visit him?"

"Absolutely not — not even if you have a relative who works in the emergency room."

"Will he be okay?" Jake ventured.

"Too early to know. The tests will say. He'll be released tomorrow if he has someone willing to stay with him for forty-eight hours after that. He mustn't be alone during that time in case he passes out again," she added. "Trouble is, he says he has no family or friends this side of the country able to be his observer."

"We could do it. All of us taking turns," Aaron suggested.

"Yeah," the other boys said.

"But you're grounded," Sandra said sternly, looking from Jake to Peter. Jake couldn't believe it. Then he saw the twinkle in her eye.

"Maybe under my supervision," she finally allowed.

The back door of the house slammed and Alyson came bolting out.

"Hi, Mom!" She slowed, a little taken aback by the sight of five boys with serious expressions.

"Hello yourself," Sandra addressed her sternly. "You, young lady, are off to the babysitter's tomorrow. I've been hearing too many rumors about what you've been up to."

"But Mom, you said...!"

"No arguments." Sandra turned to the three visitors. "Well? What are you all doing, standing there staring at me? Don't forget your skateboards, have a nice day, and may I suggest" — she paused for effect — "that you have a quiet night close to home."

Oops, thought Jake. Then he smiled. As if any of us have a drop of energy for doing anything else.

15   Final Shoot

Knowing that Gabe, Bruce, and a new rehab were going on duty at nine o'clock, Peter enjoyed the luxury of sleeping in. When Jake shook him at ten, he felt entirely capable of turning over and finishing off his dream, which had something to do with choosing an agent from a roomful of applicants.

"Peter, get up."

"Don't have to be there till noon."

"Yeah, well, we want to meet with the guys before noon, don't we?"

"Sure." He sat up slowly, rubbed his eyes. "It's sunny."

"It's been sunny for hours. Not that we care. We're going to be inside all day."

"Yeah, next sport we take up has to be outdoors."

"Peter, get moving."

The phone rang while they were eating breakfast. Peter got there first.

"Hello? Hey, Bruce, how's it going?"

"Terrible, but we're on top of it now," Bruce's voice came through the phone.

"What do you mean, terrible?" Peter saw a flicker of panic cross Jake's face.

"The air conditioner broke down in the night. It was really stuffy when we got here. I was showing Rod, the new rehab, how to mop floors while Marco was yelling at Gabe to get a repair guy in here immediately."

"And?"

"So Gabe is looking through the Yellow Pages when Rod walks over to the air conditioner, pulls tools out of his tool belt, and starts taking it apart."

"Uh-oh."

"Marco goes ballistic, screaming at the rehab, and Gabe says leave him alone, and then Rod finishes fiddling and the air conditioner starts to work."

"Whoa. Must've been an air conditioning repair guy in his former life."

"Guess so. We asked him if he'd ever fixed an air conditioner before and he says, 'I don't know.'"

"Weird. Otherwise things okay?"

"So far, so good. Marco's guys repaired the deck and it's all good."

"Jake wants to know if you'll put him on with Marco."

Peter handed the phone to Jake and listened as Jake

told Marco about Judd having ID for delivering soft drinks to the catering table. When he hung up, he turned to Peter.

"Marco is on it. He's got it in for Judd anyway, after their last performance, and he's putting extra security guards on duty."

"Good. Ready for some rad skateboarding?"

"Ready as I'll ever be."

They rolled slowly to the skatepark. Peter felt better today, after a full night's sleep. He only wished Kwasi could be there to watch the final shoot. The site was hopping as they passed through several security checks, dropped their boards in the office, and headed for the food table. Aaron was there already, plate loaded.

"Last day of free food," he said with a wink. "Gabe's been over here every ten minutes. You'd think he'd never seen food before. Or maybe he's swiping it for the new rehab, who looks like skin stretched over a skeleton."

"Kwasi says TBIs sometimes forget to eat if it's not on their list," Peter said. "Don't think I'd make a very good TBI on that count," he joked, a doughnut in each hand. "Do we have a plan?"

"Bruce, Gabe, and I are on full alert, and one of us is watching the entry points to the undersides at all times. I think that's all the plan we need."

"Any word on Kwasi?"

"They won't give out any information over the phone, and my mother hasn't been in yet today to give us an update."

"Hi, guys." It was Karl. He took a seat beside them, his plate full of fresh fruit. Peter took note: Successful actors eat fruit, not doughnuts.

"That was pretty scary yesterday. Aydin and I couldn't believe the deck caved in. I knew stunt work was dangerous, but this is the first time I've witnessed an accident. I'm glad you guys didn't get hurt, but it was rotten for the manager. Is he going to be okay?"

Peter thought it was totally decent of Karl to be concerned. "We think he's going to be okay." He wished he knew for sure.

"That's great to hear. I can't believe he uses mental patients to help with maintenance. That must worry you guys, too, eh?"

"They're supervised," Jake spoke up. Peter thought his voice sounded unnecessarily edgy.

"Karl, can you tell me how you got into acting?" Peter asked. Karl looked so much like Jake, it was hard not to feel totally comfortable around him. "And how you found an agent?" He watched Jake rise and wander away.

"No problem," Karl said with a disarming smile. "But if you're looking at an acting career, I don't mind telling you that having Marco on your side is No. 1."

Peter sat enthralled at Karl's stories and soaked in every piece of advice for half an hour. When Miranda interrupted them to remind Peter to head to the dressing room, he all but floated to the trailer on a cloud of happiness. Inside advice from a successful actor. This was going to be a great day.

"Break a leg," Karl called after him. "Hey, I'm just kidding."

In full costume and makeup, Peter grabbed his board from Kwasi's office and joined Jake and Marco on the floor. He listened closely to the sequence of tricks Marco was outlining and applied his memory techniques to make sure he remembered them. As he launched into the string of moves, he saw Bruce, Gabe, and the guy who must be Rod at the far end of the room. He knew they'd been under the ramps just minutes before. He felt confident nothing would go wrong today.

For a full hour, he and Jake skated their hearts out as cranes, dollies, and small helicopters moved around them. Jake needed a little encouragement and quiet coaching now and again, but he was holding his own and Peter was proud of him. Jake seemed a little nervous, especially on bowl tricks, but he was hiding it well.

"Excellent," Marco kept saying. "You boys are in fine form today."

Peter's hips and heels were aching by the time Marco finally called a break. "One more shoot after lunch, and it's over," he said cheerfully.

They dumped their boards in Kwasi's office, where Bruce was sitting.

"Marco won't let me play tunes," he groused, "even on lunch hour."

"That would just distract you from guard duty anyway," Peter teased. "Need a break?"

"Sure. I'll get some lunch and come straight back here. Then maybe one of you can spell Gabe and Rod."

Peter sank down in Kwasi's most comfortable chair and spun the wheels on his skateboard as he looked about. It was nice and cool in here. He spotted a book titled *Memory* and pulled it down off the shelf. It was full of big words. It was boring.

"Peter, just wanted to congratulate you on a super session," Marco said, standing in the doorway. "It has been a pleasure working with you all week, in fact. Karl tells me you might have an interest in acting. Would you like to talk about that?"

Peter sat bolt upright. "Yes, sir."

"Have you had lunch?"

"No, sir."

"Then let's see what the caterers can do for us."

Peter matched Marco's gait stride for stride. He imagined crew members treating him altogether differently after seeing him sharing lunch with the boss. Somehow, it didn't surprise him that the caterers supplied the two of them with china rather than paper plates, and served them rather than letting them serve themselves.

It was only a ten-minute conversation, and it's not like Marco promised anything, but he listened to Peter's plans, and he offered some advice on shopping for an agent. All that really mattered is that he now knew Peter's goals and had taken the time to show an interest in them. Peter could build on that later, he was certain.

When Peter returned to Kwasi's office, Gabe had taken the comfortable seat and was working his way through a giant piece of apple pie.

"Everything okay?" Peter asked.

"Yup."

"New guy working out?"

"He's like Billy. Has to have everything on a list. But he loves the tool belt."

"Good. One more hour, we'll be out of here. Coming to the hospital to pick up Kwasi?"

Gabe studied the floor. "Nope. I have to go home."

Jake had told Peter about Gabe's home.

"Have to, Gabe?"

"Going with my mom and dad somewhere. Somewhere Kwasi arranged."

"Oh." Peter knew better than to pry, but from the hint of light in Gabe's eyes, he guessed it was something that might make his home life better. *Good old Kwasi,* Peter thought: *saving the world, one skater at a time.*

Peter reached over Gabe for his board as Jake arrived to do the same.

"Okay," Marco addressed them a few minutes later, "for this last sequence, I'm needing you boys to carve and smith grind. No warm-up needed, I think. Cameras will be rolling the minute you are."

Peter gave Marco a big smile and rolled toward the lip. He dropped in and busted a smith. His board wavered a little more than he liked on the roll-up, but he felt stoked to roll away. Jake was right behind him.

He saw Bruce and Rod standing near the deck. As he neared them, he kept his eyes averted so as not to be distracted. As he ollied, the board slipped a fraction, but he recovered so smoothly that he was sure Marco wouldn't call a new take. He was about to slide when he saw Rod jump up onto the ramp. Just as fast, Bruce grabbed Rod's shirt and tried to pull him back, but the rail-thin man escaped his clutches.

Peter figured Bruce would stop the rehab on the next grab and that Rod was out of camera range. He made a quick decision to carry on, then flew up and over the ramp's lip and touched down. As his wheels hit the surface, he felt his body lurch, heard the sound of his truck breaking at one end and a wheel rolling away. His body corkscrewed trying to stay upright, then his ankle twisted, and he felt his body slam against the deck. He was sliding, sliding on his side, all the way to the bottom of the bowl. Even before he came to a halt, Peter instinctively had his hands over his face, expecting Jake to come crashing down on top of him. Instead, he felt the vibration of thuds behind him and heard the whir of Jake's skateboard speed by within an inch of his head.

Pain shot through his ankle, and he turned to see Rod kneeling on the ramp, holding Jake, face pressed against Jake's helmet. Jake's face registered shock.

"Peter, Jake, are you okay?" Marco said, rushing over. "Security, get this man under control. He's caused a terrible accident."

It was my loose wheel, not the new rehab, that caused the crash! Peter could hear the words in his head, but the scene playing out in front of him had left him without words. Rod, looking frightened of Marco, had stood up, retrieved the two runaway boards, and then bent down to pick up Peter's wheel. He squatted down on the floor a short distance away, his back to Peter, and lifted a screwdriver from his tool belt.

Only a crazy man would think this was the time and place to repair the skateboards, Peter thought, shaking his head and cupping his hands around his throbbing ankle. He looked toward Jake to see if his buddy had been hurt. Jake was so pasty-faced Peter wondered if he'd been seriously injured until his friend leapt up to block security guards from reaching Rod.

"Leave him alone. He's fixing our boards," Jake shouted, standing protectively over the crouched man.

Huh? Peter watched as Jake, eyes locked on Rod's face, gently took his own board from the rehab and lifted it above his head to demonstrate a nearly disconnected axle. "Way off its threads," he announced in a strange, choked voice. Peter wondered if he was on the verge of passing out. Then, grabbing onto Rod's shoulder as if for support, Jake steadied himself. "Funny," he continued in a louder, angrier voice, "because I tightened them up right before lunch. Just like Peter made sure his wheel nuts were tight."

Peter shook his head, trying to dispel the dreamlike quality of the scene. He *had* tightened his wheel nuts just before lunch but he couldn't believe someone would deliberately sabotage his and Jake's boards. *They could have been killed.* He tried to stand up, but his ankle gave way and he collapsed on his side. He bit his tongue as pain shot up his leg. Jake lunged at one of the security guards reaching for Rod, who was still bent over, concentrating on his task.

"You leave him alone!" Jake shouted so viciously that the room went dead silent and the guards drew back. Clutching both of Rod's shoulders now, Jake turned and looked straight at Marco. His eyes were flashing like Peter had never seen before. "Peter's board falling apart made for a heck of an action shot, didn't it, Marco? Real drama. Real pain. And on film. Yesterday's footage would have been better, except that it was Kwasi, not Karl's double who got injured. Today you would have captured two skaters going down at once, except for Rod here getting in the way. You'd like to fire him, Marco, wouldn't you? Like you fired Billy, because Rod might be able to tell us who was in the office messing with the boards during lunch. And Gabe might be able to back him up."

Way to go, Jake. Accusing the director of trying to injure his stuntboys seemed far-fetched. Something strange was definitely going down here, but would Marco seriously risk lives for some killer footage? Peter looked over at Gabe, who was standing with arms crossed, studying the crowd. Behind him, Aaron was on the phone in Kwasi's office. No one was backing Jake up. Yet.

Marco spoke. "Jake, calm down. This man is mentally challenged. He can't tell us a thing."

"Dad," Jake said, squatting down until his eyes were level with Rod's, and taking Rod's hands in his.

Peter felt a bolt go through his chest. He stared at the back of Rod's head. Then, mindless of his throbbing ankle, he rolled until he could see Rod's face. His breath ran out of him. It was Robert Evans. Fifty pounds lighter than the last time Peter had seen him, and gazing with an empty stare at his son, but it was Jake's dad.

"Dad," Jake heard himself repeating more softly as he bent down and pulled his father's leathery hands close to his own chest. He could feel his knees about to buckle as waves of emotion continued to batter him, so he kneeled and took some deep breaths. It was killing him to see no sign of recognition in his father's widened pupils.

In an effort to summon one more bout of courage, Jake turned and looked for Marco. He saw that the director's jaw had come unhinged. This steeled him to ask, loud enough for people to hear, "Dad, has anyone else been fixing these boards with tools?"

Jake's heart pounded as Robert Evans turned and looked at the circle of people pressed around him. Robert pointed at Karl. Karl began backing away. Jake, unable to choke out another word, stepped back from the unfamiliar, skeletal form of his father. He wasn't quite ready to embrace him, yet he felt highly protective of him. He barely registered the next few exchanges. His desire to keep Marco's crew away from his father was the strongest urge in a rising storm of confused feelings.

"Karl!" Marco shouted. "Have you touched Jake's and Peter's boards?"

"Of course not," Jake heard Karl say. "This guy's a lunatic, and stuntboys are in charge of their own equipment."

"But you do what Marco tells you to, don't you?" Jake looked over at Peter, who had suddenly addressed Karl from where he sat. His friend had been unusually quiet up until now. "Like you told me, your career depends on staying in with Marco," Peter continued. "And you and Jake look so much alike, it wouldn't be hard for people to mistake you under the bowls or in the office on a quick mission. But a father might know the two of you apart."

Was that true? Jake wondered, when his father still didn't seem to recognize him. He looked at Karl in time to catch his wary glance at the rehab.

"Gabe," Peter demanded, "who's been in the office touching the boards between lunch and the shoot?"

"Rod and I went into the office right after Peter left with Marco. I left Rod there for three minutes while I went to the can. When I came out, I thought it was you leaving the office. But you were under the constructions with Bruce at the time. So it had to be Karl." Even as he spoke, Gabe was staring at Jake and his rehab father in undisguised amazement.

"Marco's new career as a director depends on this movie turning out exciting," Peter was saying. "If accidents happen during shooting, well, there's no point wasting good footage, right?"

Jake was hearing, but not listening. He wanted this scene to end. He desperately wanted out of the public eye. He wanted to know if finding his father was a dream or a reality. His chest felt on the verge of exploding. But Marco still had some lines to deliver.

"Peter, listen to yourself and think what you're saying. This will do nothing for your acting career," the director said. Jake focused on the sweat trickling down Marco's face. "These are cheap accusations, boys. As a skater, I know myself how easy it is for wheels to come loose after long sessions if they haven't been tightened properly. If you've been negligent in keeping your equipment up to par, it does no good to blame others."

Others? Like my father? But Jake had lost any ability to deliver thoughts as spoken words.

"Excitement Films will pay all medical expenses for your ankle sprain, if that's what it is, Peter. We really shouldn't be wasting time talking when our first-aid staff need to get ice on it."

"Funny, you were more worried about security

staff getting hold of Rod than you were about Peter a minute ago," Aaron remarked.

This prompted Jake to help his father to his feet. Robert did not resist. Jake cast his eyes about for a place to lead the man away from this crowd. Away, and home. Home, where he, Jake, could collapse under the weight of the shock. All he wanted was to see his father crossing over the Evans's bungalow doorstep, to make this bizarre reunion real. He wanted to see happy faces on his mother and sister again. And he wanted to believe that within weeks, his father would be acting normally and life would be as it had been three years ago. Nothing else mattered.

Just then the front doors swung open. Jake saw Aaron nod at Peter as two police officers entered. "Folks, we're just asking that no one leave the building till we've located and questioned a few individuals."

A murmur ran through the crowd. Jake saw Karl and Marco exchange a look. He sighed. It was out of his and Peter's hands now, but he fiercely resented the delay in getting out of here. Could he hold it together for a few more minutes? Slowly, he led his father toward Peter, who was wincing as he maneuvered his way toward Jake and Robert on his palms, bottom, and one good heel.

"Mr. Evans," Peter said, voice a little unsteady as he held one hand up to the man, and squeezed Jake's with his other.

"I'm Peter. Peter Montpetit. Do you remember me?"

Jake held his breath.

"Nice to meet you," Robert said politely. Jake felt the first tears begin to spill; he no longer had any power to stop them. As he squeezed his eyelids shut and tried to turn away, he felt a hand touch his cheek gently.

"I know you, don't I?" his father asked in a husky voice.

Jake took a long, shaky breath and fought harder for control. "Yes, Dad, you know me," he managed. "Happy birthday four days late."

16   Family

Jake and Kwasi watched Jake's dad move around the garage, touching shelves, bottles, and tools thoughtfully. They watched him move to the quarter-pipe, still pushed together where Jake had napped on it the other day.

He ran his hand along it, then turned and studied Jake. Jake's heart ached with more emotions than he could identify, almost more than he could hold in. He hated that anger was one of them. Anger that his dad had walked out three years ago and done this to them all, including himself. Kwasi rested a steady hand on Jake's shoulder.

Jake's dad had been home now for two days. Two days, Jake reflected, was not enough to make a dent in the shock, joy, angst, and confusion that still enveloped the Evans household. But today, Jake hoped, might be a little different. Today, Kwasi was out of the hospital and spending time with them. And he had brought Jake's father's folder with him, something they'd all been waiting for.

"Give me a few minutes alone with your mother and father," Kwasi said gently.

Jake nodded. With the man Jake still thought of sometimes as "Rod" between them, they stepped out of the garage. Alyson was leaning on the railing of the back deck. Jake slowed, rested a hand on her head, and let Kwasi walk his dad into the house.

"He likes going into the garage," Alyson observed softly.

"He's trying to put things together," Jake said quietly.

"But he can't, can he?" she asked, a tear spilling down her face.

"I don't know," Jake said, for the hundredth time the past two days.

"Mom thinks he will," she said, lifting her chin and wiping an arm across her cheekbone.

Jake said nothing. What was there to say?

"I can't believe you thought Judd would sabotage the constructions," Alyson said, as if keen to change the subject.

"Sorry about that," he mumbled. He'd been expecting her to spit that out for two days now. Maybe it was a good thing to finally talk about something other than their dad's return.

"Judd and his friends would never have done anything like that, or tried to break into Sk8 again," she said, trying to sound stern. "Number one, Judd didn't really mean anything when he said Kwasi would be sorry if he didn't allow BMX seshes. He just talks mean, like Aaron and those guys. He's not really mean."

Jake stifled a smile. If there was anything he'd learned this last week, it was that neither people nor skateboard constructions are what they appear to be on the surface.

"Number two" — Alyson held up two fingers like a teacher talking to a Grade 1 class — "Kwasi told him he would let them in if they changed their pedals and pegs. And I was onto that, and they knew it, as I was trying to tell you, Jake, when you walked off." She looked at her brother.

"Okay, I'm listening now," Jake said, reaching forward to tug her braid. He realized that he hadn't tugged her braid in a couple of days. Hugged her, laughed and cried with her, but tugged her braid, no.

"And anyway, I know Judd and his friends are okay 'cause I've been around them enough." She lowered her head for a minute. "They've even been nice about Dad." She was silent for a moment. It hadn't been easy on either of them, their friends and neighbors knowing about their dad's condition. But Alyson was sticking to her topic. "I know you didn't want me to spend time with them, but I kept my promise not to let them use the half-pipe at Sam's anymore. When Billy got fired, I didn't have anyone else to teach me, and I want to be a BMXer. I am a BMXer," she said more assertively, with a pouty look at Jake. "All except for having a bike."

"Why the heck would Judd hang out with a twelve-year-old?" Jake couldn't resist asking.

Alyson crossed her arms. "At first, he taught me tricks because I let him use your half-pipe. And then it was because he knew Kwasi liked me, and I promised him I'd get Kwasi to agree to BMX time at Sk8 if he taught me a few more tricks," she said. "I know he wouldn't have even spoken to me otherwise. I'm not that dumb." She tossed her head.

Jake was torn between shaking her and hugging her. So she'd defied him again. Well, he wasn't her dad, just her brother. And she'd been sneaking around because she wanted to be a BMXer. He'd done enough sports to know how it felt to just *have* to do a sport. Even when you don't have the money for the equipment to do it.

He wrapped an arm around her shoulders, noticed how wide they'd become. "Let's go in the house."

Inside, Sandra was drying her eyes.

"Shall we start now?" Kwasi asked kindly as Jake and Alyson seated themselves.

"Yes. I'm sorry," she said.

"Robert, you're okay with me going through your file with them? You've heard all this before," Kwasi asked.

Robert nodded. He hadn't said much in two long days. Jake sensed that his father preferred listening to speaking.

"Dad, want some coffee?" Jake asked, pleased when this elicited pleasure in his father's eyes.

He busied himself pouring his dad a cup. "Still two lumps of sugar and no milk?" he asked teasingly, trying to lighten the mood.

His father smiled and held up two fingers, like he always had, even before he'd left them. Jake plopped two sugar cubes into his dad's coffee and walked the steaming cup from the kitchen counter to his dad's place at the table. He waited for the slow smile that always came next. Then he reached down and hugged his dad hard, which widened the grin and, for the first time, prompted a return hug.

"You're my son," Robert said, like a child repeating lines taught by a drama teacher.

"I'm your son," Jake confirmed, more patiently and with more happiness than he had felt in days.

Kwasi smiled and reached for a thick file on top of his briefcase. Then his expression became serious and he spoke slowly, like a doctor delivering weighty news.

"He was picked up by ambulance at nine p.m. on August 22nd three years ago."

"The day after his birthday," Alyson said soberly.

"The day after he left here," said Sandra, wiping a hand across her eyes again.

"In Saskatoon, Saskatchewan," Kwasi continued.

"That's nearly a thousand miles!" Sandra exclaimed.

"He must have caught an overnight ride with a truck driver to have covered that much ground," Kwasi speculated. "He was hitchhiking outside Saskatoon. The car didn't see him in time. It threw him thirty feet."

Sandra blew her nose. Robert lifted a finger to her eyes and brushed a tear away.

"I'm sorry. I remember nothing of this," he said apologetically.

"It's okay, Dad," Jake said, reaching for his hand and squeezing it. Every day, it was getting a little easier to say that, he realized.

"He had no wallet or other identification on him, only the clothes on his back. He was unconscious for two and a half days, and on life support for part of that. He rated low on the Glasgow-Coma scale for vital signs."

"Speak English, Kwasi," Jake spoke up.

"That means he was in a mild coma. When he came to, he was moved to an intensive care unit for a week. He thought his name was Rod." Kwasi briefly scanned Robert's face. "Right, Robert?" he asked quietly, eliciting another sober nod.

"Because it sounds like Rob," Sandra said, voice breaking and reaching for her husband's hand, which he gave her willingly.

"He was unable to recall his last name. We call that a John Doe case."

Sandra nodded. Jake looked at Alyson. She looked ready to start crying again. He pulled her chair closer to him.

"After eight weeks in a neurosurgical unit, he went to a rehab program, where he has been since. He couldn't remember his name or any other details of his previous life, but he recently insisted he had lived in British Columbia. That, after considerable red tape, led to his transfer here, in hopes it might further tweak his memory or help us locate relatives.

"Most patients with retrograde amnesia recover whatever memory they're going to recover within the first few months. Some take two years. Robert is a moderately severe case. He's also what they call 'slow to recover.' He's still regaining memory, but in small increments."

Alyson squirmed beside Jake. "Kwasi, do you think he'll ever fully recover?"

Kwasi's long arm reached out and rested on

Alyson's head. "Alyson, no one ever fully recovers from a traumatic brain injury."

Jake shot a look at his dad. He looked unfazed, like he'd been told that lots of times. *I need to accept it like he and Kwasi have,* Jake thought to himself.

"If he lives at home here, will that help?" Jake asked, proud that his mother was holding herself together okay.

"Home support has been known to accelerate rehabilitation. It's an unknown, Jake, but in my heart, I believe it will help in this case." He was looking at Robert, whose eyes were soberly scanning the faces of his family, one by one, as if trying to match the images before him with torn and faded pictures in a scrapbook.

Jake felt himself getting restless. He appreciated Kwasi's kindness, but he needed a break from his mother's pain, his father's confusion, and Alyson's need for a strong brother.

"We're pretty much finished, Jake, if you want to stretch your legs," Kwasi said.

"Jake, you've hardly been out of this house for days. Take an hour off. We're okay," his mother said.

Jake looked at Alyson. "Get out of here," she joked.

"Thanks," Jake said. "I'm going to catch some air." He lifted his backpack from the coat hook near the back door.

"Be home by supper," came a familiar voice from

the table. Jake spun around, felt his heart skip a beat as he realized his dad had spoken. He saw his mother smile, and Alyson crawl into her dad's lap.

Kwasi laughed. "So go."

As he exited, Jake realized his skateboard was hanging from the backpack like a neglected friend. His bike was resting against the back fence. He climbed on and rode where the tires seemed to take him. It was a cool evening. Fall weather was moving in. School was starting Monday. It was the end of a long summer. Jake missed Peter, who'd returned to Seattle. No doubt the crutches would garner him lots of attention, which he wouldn't mind a bit. Before he'd left, he'd spent a little time with the Evanses, humoring Robert Evans in a way they all needed to learn to do more effectively. He'd also confessed to Jake that he had decided against being an actor.

"Why?" Jake had asked.

"Too shallow," he'd replied.

"Then be like Kwasi," Jake had suggested. "Turn an ordinary job into something that counts."

"Hadn't thought of that," Peter had replied with a studied nonchalance.

Marco's case would be under investigation for some time, Jake had been told. He didn't care. All that mattered was Kwasi was okay so far — would hopefully be diagnosed as having no brain damage. And his father was home: a mystery to unravel and support, a stranger to help rehabilitate. But Jake wasn't afraid of rehabs anymore. And he wasn't alone in his task. Gabe, now "assistant manager" of the park, if one took any stock in Kwasi's big words, was helping to bring Robert along. So was Billy, who seemed to have buckled down under the influence of Robert's hardworking example, now that he'd been given a second chance.

As for Aaron and Bruce, well, they were still pulling pranks on Kwasi's rehabs, but harmless pranks. Come to think of it, they always had been harmless, Jake reflected. Like Jake and Alyson, they did just enough chores around Sk8 to qualify for a half-price membership. And Alyson had finally convinced Kwasi to turn Sk8 over to BMXers one afternoon each week.

As Jake's tires entered a quiet, tree-lined street along the river, he squinted at a certain bank of nine concrete steps. His bike took the grassy slope to the pavement above them, and parked itself outside Sam's Adventure Tours' garage. The skateboard unbuckled itself, dropped to the ground, and positioned itself under his feet.

As he began to roll down the walkway, he couldn't believe he'd ever been nervous of a couple of concrete steps. With a relaxed body shift, he took flight, knowing the board would stay connected with his shoes. He peered down as he sailed over the last step, curious whether the gnome still lived there. *Ha!* he thought: No sign of the mischief-maker. But as his wheels touched down effortlessly, he imagined the little fellow beneath a faraway tree, winking and giving him a thumbs up before turning and wandering off in search of a better hangout.

"Looks like you're ready to go pro," a woman's voice floated down to him through the evening air, "no thanks to time spent on that beautiful, abandoned half-pipe in Sam's backyard. But we don't mind. We just look on it as an interesting sculpture, donated by a notable artist."

Jake smiled at Nancy.

"Now, all that stuntboy pay, Jake." She suddenly looked concerned. "You will get paid, won't you?"

"Have been already. Miranda, Marco's assistant, dropped the checks off after the final shoot."

"Good for her. So, where are you going to spend it? I hope you're not feeling so rich that you're going to quit Sam's Adventure Tours."

"Not likely," he returned. "Most of it will be gone by tomorrow." He was amused at the surprised look that crossed his boss's face. "On a used BMX bike. For Alyson."

Nancy moved to a beam of sunlight creeping onto Sam's front porch. "Now, why doesn't that surprise me?"

Jake, still smiling, shrugged. "You should drop into Xtreme Sk8 sometime, Nancy. Come watch some real skateboarding action."

"As a matter of fact, I plan to," she replied, stretching her long legs in front of her on Sam's front steps and tossing her long, dark hair. "That way I can say hi to your dad, too. Been a long time."

"Uh-huh."

"I hear he's been busy training the rest of the crew." She paused and her brow creased. "What is it exactly that Sk8's maintenance guys do, Jake?"

Jake popped his board up to his hand and plopped down beside her. "They tighten screws, mop floors with cola, and clean loogies off the wall."

"Loogies?"

"Trust me, Nancy. It's something you'll never need to know."

Acknowledgements

I was delighted to work closely with Kevin Kelly on this book. A skateboarder since 1986, he has instructed more than three thousand children and organized more than forty skateboard events, ranging from Skate It Up and Ambush to Slam City Jam. He is also president of the Vancouver Skateboard Coalition. Kevin was part of this novel from the start: He helped shape the overall plot, he "choreographed" all the action scenes, and he helped me punch up the skaters' dialog. He even spent time touring me around the undersides of an indoor skatepark, explaining construction technique and sabotage possibilities.

I'd also like to thank Brock Watson, my teen skateboarder reader; Chuck Lawson, backyard half-pipe builder; Ron Stewart, special effects assistant and scriptwriter for feature films and television; Peter Dawson, program coordinator with the B.C. Neuropsychiatry Program at the University of British Columbia Hospital; Larraine Michaelson, RN; Peter Moffat, who "helped Jake" fix Kwasi's car; and my friend Ken Gikunda, who named Kwasi. (Minus the skateboard and dreadlocks, I based Kwasi on my father, the most dedicated youth worker I know.)

Very special thanks to Hui Lim, occupational therapist and program coordinator with the Lower Mainland Brain Injury Association in Vancouver, Canada, who read the entire novel and helped vet the "TBIs" in it.

I'd also like to pay tribute to two books: *Over My Head: A Doctor's Own Story of Head Injury from the Inside Looking Out* by Claudia L. Osborn (Andrews/McMeel Publishing, 1998); and Peter's memory tricks book: *Memory Techniques in a Week* by Jonathan Hancock and Cheryl Buggy (Hodder & Stoughton, 1999).

Finally, as always, thanks to my son Jeremy Withers, the most astute teen editor I'll ever have; to all the Whitecap Books staff; to my agent, Leona Trainer; and to my speaking tours agent, Chris Patrick.

About the Author

Pam Withers has worked as a journalist, editor, and associate publisher. She is also a former outdoor guide who ran a summer camp for teens for many years. She lives in Vancouver, British Columbia, Canada — a popular skateboard mecca — with her husband and teenaged son, where she enjoys sports when she's not writing and editing books or touring North America to speak in schools.

Look for the next book in the *Take It to the Xtreme* series, when a scuba-diving misadventure leaves Jake, Peter, and a surfer girl stranded on an island from which surfboards offer the only escape. For more information on the series, to write Pam, or to book her as a speaker, check out www.TakeItToTheXtreme.com.

ISBN 1-55285-510-4

Arch rivals and sometimes friends Peter and Jake are delighted to be part of a whitewater-rafting trip. But after a series of disasters leaves the group stranded in the wilderness, it's up to them to confront the dangerous rapids to search for help. This is the first title in the extreme outdoor sports series by Pam Withers.

Jake, Peter, and Moses are looking forward to heli-skiing and snowboarding in the backcountry near Whistler. But just after they're dropped off on a mountain peak, bad weather closes in and a helicopter crashes. It's up to them to rescue any survivors and overcome avalanches, hypothermia, and wild animals to make their way to safety.

ISBN 1-55285-530-9

ISBN 1-55285-604-6

It's summer vacation for best friends Peter and Jake, and when they're invited to help develop a mountain bike trail west of the Canadian Rockies, they can't believe their luck. But as they start working hard in an isolated park, the boys sense that something's not right. Join the boys as they plunge into the mountain-biking descent of their lives.

Fifteen-year-olds Jake and Peter land jobs as skateboarding stuntboys on a movie set. The boys couldn't be happier, but their dream job proves to be more trouble than they expected. A demanding director, an uneasy relationship with three local skateboarding toughs, and a sabotage attempt —which suggests a jealous rival in their midst—are just some of the obstacles these stuntboys encounter.

ISBN 1-55285-647-X

A scuba-diving accident leaves Jake and Peter and a surfer girl stranded on a deserted island with surfboards as their only means of escape. The storm of the century is fast approaching, and the boys need to think fast if they're going to get home in one piece. This adrenalin-pumping book is sure to keep readers on the edge of their seats.

ISBN 1-55285-718-2

Jake is obsessed with solo-climbing a soaring granite spire. Peter is as absorbed with filming Jake for a video as he is in not divulging his secret fear of heights to the runaway girl who joins them.

During the climb, all seems well, but the next day, a lightening storm begins to unravel the adventure. Whefn a crisis prompts the girl to put her life at stake for Jake, Peter must overcome his fear to get everyone home safely.

ISBN 1-55285-783-2

The charitable, non-profit Tony Hawk Foundation was established to promote and provide funds for high-quality public skateboard parks in low-income areas. Since its launch in 2002, the foundation has given away over 1 million dollars to more than 250 skatepark projects.

Most cities have no experience building skateboard parks. As a result, far too many end up producing unskateable parks with kinky transitions and cluttered designs that contribute to collisions and injuries. Tony's foundation favors projects in which local skaters have been involved on a grassroots level, and that plan to hire experienced skatepark builders.

The foundation was established by a gift from Tony, who continues to donate some of his public appearance fees. Significant contributions have also been made by our corporate sponsors and other private donors. In addition, the foundation receives a portion of the proceeds from Tony's Boom Boom HuckJam national arena tour.

For more information, please visit our website at www.tonyhawkfoundation.org